I0740973

CHARACTERS
(In Order of Speaking)

DAREDEVILETTE #1 . . . . *vocalist*

DAREDEVILETTE #2 . . . . *vocalist*

DAREDEVILETTE #3 . . . . *vocalist*

RADIO ANNOUNCER . . . . *for Amazing Adventures*

DAN DAREDEVIL . . . . . . *America's number one radio hero*

BETTY PARKER. . . . . *Dan's longtime friend*

MURDOCK. . . . . *Criminal mastermind, also known as "The Fog"*

ADAM. . . . . *robot*

LORELEI . . . . *maid, excitable*

MRS. HERRINGBONE . . . . *sinister housekeeper*

CAP'N SCAR . . . . *modern day pirate*

NYOKA STERLING. . . . . *nosy neighbor*

PHILO. . . . . *Betty's uncle*

COUNTESS FREDERIKA . . . . *foreign agent, beautiful but evil*

CHARACTERS
(continued)

ANYANKA . . . .*forbidden cargo*

OPTIONAL EXTRAS . . . *more forbidden cargo, government
agents*

and
WOOF, The Wonder Dog

The Amazing Adventures of Dan Daredevil

A Musical Spoof of Radio's Golden Age

Book by Tim Kelly
Music by Arne Christiansen
Lyrics by Ole Kittleson

Single copies of plays are sold for reading purposes only. The copying or duplicating of a play, or any part of play, by hand or by any other process, is an infringement of the copyright. Such infringement will be vigorously prosecuted.

Baker's Plays
7611 Sunset Blvd.
Los Angeles, CA 90042
bakersplays.com

NOTICE

This book is offered for sale at the price quoted only on the understanding that, if any additional copies of the whole or any part are necessary for its production, such additional copies will be purchased. The attention of all purchasers is directed to the following: this work is fully protected under the copyright laws of the United States of America, the British Commonwealth, including Canada, and all other countries of the Copyright Union. Violations of the Copyright Law are punishable by fine or imprisonment, or both. The copying or duplication of this work or any part of this work, by hand or by any process, is an infringement of the copyright and will be vigorously prosecuted.

This play may not be produced by amateurs or professionals for public or private performance without first submitting application for performing rights. Licensing fees are due on all performances whether for charity or gain, or whether admission is charged or not. Since performance of this play without the payment of the licensing fee renders anybody participating liable to severe penalties imposed by the law, anybody acting in this play should be sure, before doing so, that the licensing fee has been paid. Professional rights, reading rights, radio broadcasting, television and all mechanical rights, etc. are strictly reserved. Application for performing rights should be made directly to BAKER'S PLAYS.

No one shall commit or authorize any act or omission by which the copyright of, or the right to copyright, this play may be impaired. No one shall make any changes in this play for the purpose of production.

Publication of this play does not imply availability for performance. Both amateurs and professionals considering a production are strongly advised in their own interest to apply to Baker's Plays for written permission before starting rehearsals, advertising, or booking a theatre.

Whenever the play is produced, the author's name must be carried in all publicity, advertising and programs. Also, the following notice must appear on all printed programs, "Produced by special arrangement with Baker's Plays."

Licensing fees for THE AMAZING ADVENTURES OF DAN DARE-DEVIL are based on a per performance rate and payable one week in advance of the production.

Please consult the Baker's Plays website at www.bakersplays.com or our current print catalogue for up to date licensing fee information.

Copyright © 1989 by Tim Kelly, Arne Christiansen, Ole Kittleson
Made in U.S.A.
All rights reserved.

THE AMAZING ADVENTURES OF DAN DAREDEVIL
ISBN **978-0-87440-095-3**
#3138-B

SYNOPSIS

A broadcasting studio in "Radio City",
Rockefeller Center, New York

Circa 1950

ACT ONE

Another episode in "The Amazing Adventures
of Dan Daredevil"

ACT TWO

The episode continues.

MUSICAL NUMBERS

OVERTURE

ACT ONE

DAN DAREDEVIL . . . . Daredevilettes

CRUNCHY CHEWS . . . . Daredevilettes

NEVER FEAR . . . . Dan, Betty, Announcer

THINK LIKE A SHARK . . . Murdock, Mrs. Herringbone, Lorelei

MAKE YOURSELF AT HOME, MY DEAR . . . Murdock, Mrs. Herringbone, Nyoka, Lorelei, Dan, Betty

THE THRILL OF IT ALL . . . . Dan

ENTR'ACTE

ACT TWO

CRUNCHY CHEWS (reprise) . . . . Daredevilettes

A BASKET OF GOODIES. . . . . Nyoka, Dan, Betty

TRAVELLERS WITHOUT PASSPORTS. . . Cap'n Scar, Anyanka

YOU'D BETTER TELL. . . Murdock, Mrs. Herringbone, Lorelei, Philo, Cap'n Scar

STRANGE MUSIC IN MY HEART . . . Countess Frederika

THE DAN DAREDEVIL CREED. . . . . Company

THE AMAZING ADVENTURES OF DAN DAREDEVIL

ACT I

EXTREME DOWN LEFT, partially on the forestage, is the broadcasting studio. There's a standing microphone. The rest of the stage represents where the radio program's imagined action will take place.

EXTREME DOWN RIGHT, partially on the FORESTAGE, is a cutout rock to suggest the top of a cliff.

Most of the stage picture is occupied by Nightmare Castle, a mausoleum well suited to shrouded figures and banging shutters. UPSTAGE CENTER there's an archway or entry that leads into the main room. Behind the archway is a hallway. RIGHT from the hallway leads to the front door. LEFT from the hallway leads to other areas of the gloomy place, including the kitchen. There are some optional stairs, or a step unit, that lead to the upper stories.

The room: DOWN RIGHT leads to the cellar. STAGE RIGHT is a standing blackboard. RIGHT CENTER is a desk and chair. Another chair is in front of the desk, angled to audience view. UP RIGHT CENTER is a standing dressing or decorative screen.

Behind the screen, high enough to conceal a person, is a table or hooks for costume changes. The screen masks a small EXIT that leads into the hallway. There's a rug CENTER. A sofa, chaise lounge or chair arrangement, is LEFT CENTER with a small table to the LEFT. STAGE LEFT has a window that looks out onto the bleak landscape. Another EXIT is LEFT, below the window. To these basics can be added anything desired to enforce the moody (and threatening) atmosphere. Some ancient lamps, a bookcase of musty volumes, fireplace, another chair, standing skeleton. (NOTE: For various suggestions on elaborating on the set, CONSULT PRODUCTION NOTES)

When OVERTURE ENDS, in the darkness of the theatre, we hear several LOUD, FAST SOUND EFFECTS. For example: A WOMAN'S SCREAM, GUNFIRE, RUSHING TRAIN, INSANE LAUGHTER, EXPLOSION, POLICE WHISTLE — anything that suggests dangerous adventure. As the SOUND EFFECTS FADE UNDER AND OUT, we hear the enthusiastic VOICES of the DAREDEVILETTES and ANNOUNCER.

DAREDEVILETTES. *(ECHOING and REVERBERATING)* Dan Daredevil, Dan Daredevil, Dan Daredevil...

ANNOUNCER. Yes, indeed, radio fans of excitement and thrills — it's time for another episode in The Amazzzzz-ing Adventures of Dan Daredevil, America's number one hero! *(LIGHTS HAVE COME UP on the radio studio, and we see ANNOUNCER at the microphone, script in hand. He has a good voice and a stylish delivery. His diction and pronunciation are somewhat overdone. To one side, or standing behind him, are three female vocalists: THE DAREDEVILETTES. [NOTE: Only the radio studio is in the LIGHT. Rest of STAGE remains in the*

SHADOWS.] ANNOUNCER steps aside so the vocalists can "take the mike")

[Music: DAN DAREDEVIL THEME SONG]

DAREDEVILETTES.
WHO IS EV'RYBODY'S HERO?
DAN DAREDEVIL BRAVE AND BOLD.
GALLANT, LOYAL AND COURAGEOUS
HE'S THE INSPIRATION OF THE NATION.
STANDING TALL FOR TRUTH AND HONOR
EACH INJUSTICE HE'LL DESTROY.
HE'S OUR FAV'RITE SON, HE IS "NUMBER ONE"
HE'S AMERICA'S PRIDE AND JOY.
(ANNOUNCER takes mike as DAREDEVILETTES step back)

ANNOUNCER. Thank you, Daredevilettes, for reminding us, once again, that Dan Daredevil is, indeed, an *amazzzzzing young man. (Looks up)* I can see by the clock on the wall it's time to recite *The Dan Daredevil Creed. (Puts his hand over his heart. Same business for DAREDEVILETTES. They recite with great feeling)*

ALL. The Dan Daredevil Creed — "I dedicate my life to the protection of all my countrymen wherever they may be. My battle is against evil. The whole purpose of my life is watching out for the little guy." *(End of Creed. Hands off hearts)* And for all you small listeners out there in radio land, Dan Daredevil reminds you: "Always follow the advice of your mom and dad." *(Excitedly)* In just a few moments, fans, I'll tell you how to get your Dan Daredevil invisibility ring and secret decoder. Get your paper and pencil ready. But first — a message from our sponsor, Crunchy Chews, the dog food that's ideal for beast or man.

[Music: CRUNCHY CHEWS]

DAREDEVILETTES.
CRUNCHY CHEWY!
CHEWY CRUNCHY!
CRUNCHY CHEWY!
CHEWY CRUNCHY!
CRUNCHY CHEWY!
CHEWY CRUNCHY!
CRUNCHY CHEWS!
OH, DAN AND WOOF, THE WONDER DOG, HAVE GOT A HUNCH.
THEY KNOW YOU'LL LOVE THE DOG FOOD WITH A LOT OF PUNCH.
THEY EAT IT EV'RY DAY AT BREAKFAST-TIME AND LUNCH.
YOU'LL LOVE CRUNCHY CHEWS A DOG-GONE BUNCH!
ANNOUNCER. WOOF! *(Again, ANNOUNCER takes mike DEVILETTES step back)* Thank you, Daredevilettes. *(Serious)* You'll remember, radio fans, when we last saw Dan, he had agreed to accompany his longtime friend, pretty Betty Parker, on a visit to her strange Uncle Philo, a scientist who lived in a strange house on a strange cliff overlooking the sea. *(DAREDEVILETTES gasp at the implications)* Dan Daredevil didn't know what he was getting into, but one thing was clear. He was heading for

danger, not running from it. *(Shift in mood)* In just a few moments, those details on the invisibility ring and secret decoder. But now, it's time for another *Amazzzzzing* Adventures of—

ALL. *(Echoing and reverberating)* Dan Daredevil, Dan Daredevil, Dan Daredevil ... *(LIGHTS FADE on radio studio. DAREDEVILETTES EXIT.*

[NOTE: What the actual theatre audience "sees" is what the imagined radio audience "hears." Therein lies much of the fun. Don't be subtle. the cornier the better.] SOUND: AIR-PLANE ENGINE HUMMING. DOWN CENTER, LIGHT-ING PICKS OUT a small, open plane [cartoon] made of cardboard or plywood. DAN is pilot. BETTY sits behind him. They both wear goggles and long red aviator scarves which are starched to look as if they are being blown about the wind. SOUND EFFECT FADES under dialogue)

DAN. Not too windy back there, Betty?

BETTY. I'm fine. don't worry about me. I certainly appreciate this, Dan.

DAN. My pleasure, Betty. What are friends for?

BETTY. I have a terrible feeling something is wrong with Uncle Philo.

DAN. How do you mean?

BETTY. It's just a feeling I have.

DAN. You probably have a touch of airsickness. The altitude.

BETTY. Uncle Philo is an unusual man. I haven't seen him since I was a child. What a surprise to get a letter from him.

DAN. Scientists are private people, Betty. To outsiders looking in, they're strange, but to insiders looking out, they're perfectly normal. *(BETTY looks dumbly into audience. Didn't understand a word)*

ANNOUNCER. *(Into mike)* Woof! Woof! Woof!

BETTY. Gosh, Dan, do you think it was a good idea to take along Woof?

ANNOUNCER. *(Into mike)* Woof! Woof! Woof! *(Supposedly, WOOF is seated beside DAN)*

DAN. Easy, boy, easy. *(To BETTY)* You know I never go anywhere without Woof, The Wonder Dog.

BETTY. I forgot. Forgive me, Woof.

ANNOUNCER. *(Into mike)* Woof.

BETTY. Did I tell you what people call my uncle's house?

DAN. Yeah. Nightmare Castle.

BETTY. I wonder why Uncle Philo wants to see me, after all these years?

DAN. *(Check dial)* We'll know soon enough. We'll be hitting the ground in about three minutes.

BETTY. So soon?

DAN. Yeah. I forgot to fill up the tank. We're almost out of fuel.

BETTY. Oh, Dan! This could be serious!

ANNOUNCER. Woof! Woof! Woof!

[Music: NEVER FEAR]

DAN.

THOUGH WE'RE FLYING THROUGH A STORM
AND THOUGH THE WEATHER SEEMS TO BE A BIT
   SEVERE

NEVER FEAR!
THOUGH YOU SEE THE LIGHTNING FLASH
AND THOUGH YOU HEAR THE THUNDER CLAP-
  PING IN YOUR EAR
NEVER FEAR!
THOUGH THE ENGINE STARTS TO STALL
AND THE PLANE BEGINS TO FALL
AND IT SEEMS AS THOUGH THE END IS VERY
  NEAR
THOUGH THE RADIO'S ERRATIC
AND I'M GETTING ONLY STATIC
  ANNOUNCER.
WOOF!
  DAN.
DAN DAREDEVIL'S HERE, SO NEVER FEAR!

  BETTY. *(Speaking as musical vamp plays under)* Dan, I'm worried. There's a big hole in the fuselage and ice is forming on the wings!

  DAN. *(Reassuring her)* Nothing serious, Betty. No-matter-what, as long as I'm in charge there's nothing to worry about. Right, boy?

  ANNOUNCER. WOOF!

  DAN. *(Singing)*
THOUGH THE TANK IS OUT OF GAS
AND THOUGH IT SEEMS AS IF WE'VE LOST THE
  LANDING GEAR
  BETTY.
NEVER FEAR!
  ANNOUNCER.
WOOF!
  BETTY.
THOUGH THE COMPASS DOESN'T WORK

AND THOUGH I SEE THAT SMOKE IS POURING
  FROM THE REAR
Dan.
NEVER FEAR!
  Announcer.
WOOF!
  Betty.
THOUGH IT REALLY IS A SHAME
THAT THE ENGINE IS AFLAME
AND IT SEEMS AS THOUGH THE END IS VERY
  NEAR

  Dan.
THE PROPELLER ISN'T SPINNING
BUT IT'S NOT THE FINAL INNING
  Announcer.
WOOF!
  Dan.
DAN DAREDEVIL'S HERE, SO NEVER FEAR!
  Betty.
NOW THE FOG IS ROLLING IN
AND THE PLANE BEGINS TO SPIN
  Dan & Betty.
AND IT SEEMS AS THOUGH THE END IS VERY
  NEAR
BOTH THE CAPTAIN AND HIS CREW
KNOW EXATLY WHAT TO DO
DAN DAREDEVIL'S HERE
  Announcer. *(Howls)*
WOOOOOOOOOOOOOOOOOOOOOOOOF!
  Dan & Betty.
NEVER FEAR!

*(BLACKOUT. SOUND OF AIRPLAINE ENGINE ROARS OUT, GRADUALLY FADES. [*Alternate suggestion: *SOUND OF PLANE GOING INTO TAILSPIN AND CRASHING ON IMPACT] In the darkness, DAN and BETTY "WALK OFF" the prop plane, RIGHT. ANNOUNCER EXITS.*

LIGHTS UP on Nightmare Castle. Seated at the desk is a dangerous criminal who calls himself THE FOG. Shortly, he will have to impersonate PHILO MURDOCK, BETTY'S flaky uncle. So, to avoid confusion in the script, The Fog will be assigned the character name of MURDOCK, while the "real" uncle will be listed as PHILO. MURDOCK is studying blueprints)

MURDOCK. Neutral atoms ... ionized gas ... one volt equal to fixed frequency ... danger of particle collision ... average energy ... yes, yes ... *(As MURDOCK babbles on with the pseudo-scientific mumbo-jumbo, a weird "thing" CLUNKS INTO VIEW UP CENTER from the hallway, LEFT. This is ADAM THE ROBOT and he's a stupid-looking pile of junk [CONSULT PRODUCTION NOTES]. ADAM walks with all the grace of a mobile saucepan. His movements are clumsy and mechanical, but he manages to move fast enough to get where he's going. To emphasize ADAM'S movement, ANNOUNCER RETURNS to the microphone with a string of tin cans. He rattles the tin cans so the radio audience can "hear" ADAM thumping about. ADAM doesn't quite know where he's going, looks LEFT and RIGHT. MURDOCK doesn't notice the robot because he's completely absorbed with the blueprints)* ... glow arc transition ... reconsider the growth factor ... electric field strength ... hmmm, hmmm ... *(ADAM plainly would like some conversation — or something — from MURDOCK. He takes a labored step to the desk. MURDOCK doesn't notice)* ... breakdown voltage must be plotted ... beware of spark plug damage ... negative pull ... hmmm, hmmm ... hubcap factor ... *(We hear LORELEI SINGING some popular tune from OFFSTAGE LEFT. ADAM stands perfectly still, then he cocks his head to one side. Listens. He decides to track down the song's source. He CLANKS OUT, LEFT. ANNOUNCER continues to work the tin cans until ADAM has made his EXIT. Then, ANNOUNCER EXITS. MURDOCK gets up and steps to blackboard with a piece of chalk and begins to draw lines, write numbers — all supposedly belonging to some electrical "formula")* Put "A" here ... "B" here ... "E" over "HG" ... "CM times NK" ... H2O ... *(SCREAM from OFFSTAGE, DOWN LEFT. LORELEI, the maid, runs IN. Starched white cap, apron)*

LORELEI. He's loose again!

MURDOCK. *(Still working out the formula)* Front disc ... rear disc ... oil change...

LORELEI. Do something!

MURDOCK. C plus C, forget about V...

LORELEI. *(Nervous glance over her shoulder)* Didn't you hear me!

MURDOCK. *(Exasperated by this interruption, MURDOCK slaps down the chalk and spins around)* Drat! You silly girl. Didn't you see I was concentrating? You interrupted my pseudo-scientific calculations.

LORELEI. *(Indeed, LORELEI is silly. Or, at least, excessively emotional. She overreacts to almost everything and she's a dim bulb)* You said you were going to keep him locked up!

MURDOCK. Who?

LORELEI. Who! Him! It! the robot!

MURDOCK. You mean Adam.

LORELEI. You can call him Adam if you want. To me, he's nothing but a walking pile of junk. He scares me.

MURDOCK. Everything scares you.

LORELEI. Can I help it if I'm a coward?

MURDOCK. I'm trying to humanize Adam.

LORELEI. Why don't you lock him up, instead.

MURDOCK. How can I humanize him if he's locked up?

LORELEI. Why ask me? I don't know anything about robots. I don't want to know. *(LORELEI is getting more and more distressed. Pulls at her cap, her apron, her hair)* I mean, it's not natural, is it? A cat I could understand. Or a dog. A hamster. Or a parakeet — but a robot? No, no, no. I don't like it.

MURDOCK. What you like or do not like is unimportant. I didn't invent the robot. That was your precious "Professor."

LORELEI. He knew how to control the thing. He didn't let it wander all over the place.

MURDOCK. I'll learn how to control it.

LORELEI. It's nothing but a trash can with batteries! *(As LORELEI babbles on and on, the sinister housekeeper, MRS. HERRINGBONE, ENTERS the hallway from LEFT. She stands perfectly still like a grim bit of graveyard statuary, her eyes focused on LORELEI. She wears a long, dark dress)* He's always popping in and out, scaring me. When he goes up and down the stairs, it's worse. Clang, clang clang. I can't sleep nights. *(Working herself into a frenzied state)* I can't stand it, I tell you! Either he goes, or I go!

MURDOCK. Calm yourself.

LORELEI. No! No! No!

MURDOCK. I'll fix you! *(Pulls a whip from a desk drawer. Holds it up, growls)* A taste of the lash!

LORELEI. *(Cowers)* No, no, no! *(ANNOUNCER ENTERS, stands at mike)*

MRS. HERRINGBONE. *(To MURDOCK)* Leave her to me. *(To LORELEI)* Enough, Lorelei. *(LORELEI continues with her hysterics. MRS. HERRINGBONE marches toward her)*

LORELEI. It's too much! A walking tomato can! It's against nature. No, no, no!

MRS. HERRINGBONE. Enough, I say! *(She SLAPS LORELEI — only she "really" doesn't. As she brings her open palm to LORELEI'S face, it's the ANNOUNCER, as sound effects person, who creates the* smack *by slapping his hands together)*

LORELEI. *(Overreacts)* Oh! You hit me!

MRS. HERRINGBONE. To teach you a lesson, my girl. *(Another "slap." Repeat ANNOUNCER business)*

LORELEI. Oh! *(MRS. HERRINGBONE makes a fist and goes for LORELEI'S mid-section)*

ANNOUNCER. *Pow!*

LORELEI. Oh! *(LORELEI doubles up. MRS. HERRINGBONE goes for the nape of the neck with her fist. ANNOUNCER creates this "sound" by slapping his own fist into the open palm of his other hand. LORELEI drops to the floor. Almost as soon as she hits, she gets up. Adjusts her cap, apron. Her manner, now, is calm and controlled)* It's you, Mrs. Herringbone. I didn't see you standing there.

MRS. HERRINGBONE. You were having another one of your — "fits." *(Motherly)* I did what I could.

MURDOCK. You must get over your fear of Adam.

MRS. HERRINGBONE. You're too emotional, Lorelei.

LORELEI. I think I made a mistake.

MURDOCK. *(Leery)* How do you mean?

LORELEI. Agreeing to help you. I think I ought to go to the police.

MURDOCK & MRS. HERRINGBONE. Police!

LORELEI. Yes, the police.

MURDOCK. Grab her, Mrs. Herringbone. *(MRS. HERRINGBONE grabs LORELEI from behind, a hammerlock)*

MRS. HERRINGBONE. I've got her. *(MURDOCK puts down the whip and steps to the UPSTAGE side of the rug. He gets down on one knee, picks up the rug and pretends to open a trapdoor — naturally, the trapdoor is blocked from audience view)*

MURDOCK. Handy things, trapdoors. Hee, hee, hee. *[NOTE: If you place a fairly large piece of wood under the rug and lift it with the carpet, it helps with the "trapdoor" illusion]*

LORELEI. Not the trapdoor!

MURDOCK. Hee, hee, hee.

LORELEI. Don't laugh like that. You make me nervous. *(MRS. HERRINGBONE pulls LORELEI to the "trapdoor")*

MURDOCK. Look below, Lorelei. There's a new pet. See what's swimming in the tank.

MRS. HERRINGBONE. Ha, ha, ha. *(ANNOUNCER makes gnashing sounds with his teeth — like aquatic growls and snarls. Or — he can pick up a large bottle which is partially filled with water, and slosh it about in front of the mike — to suggest that "something" is swimming in the tank)*

MURDOCK. Back and forth it swims. Such pearly white teeth. What a wicked smile. Look!

LORELEI. *(Innocently)* I'll take your word for it.

MRS. HERRINGBONE. You heard him. Look! *(More aquatic sounds. Sheepishly, LORELEI looks)*

LORELEI. That's not the professor's pet porpoise!

MURDOCK. You're telling me. *(ANNOUNCER EXITS)*
LORELEI. What is that thing?
MURDOCK. *(Grins)* It ain't a Maine lobster.
MRS. HERRINGBONE. It's a shark.
LORELEI. *(Terrified)* Shark! I promise I'll be good!
MURDOCK. You'd better be. *(He shuts the trap. Drops the rug back into place, stands)*
MRS. HERRINGBONE. Like you, Lorelei, the shark also gets nervous.
LORELEI. *(Leery)* It does?
MURDOCK. Oh, yes.
MRS. HERRINGBONE. Especially when it hasn't eaten in days and days. Especially when it smells "food."
LORELEI. Food? What ... what ... what happened to the porpoise?
MURDOCK & MRS. HERRINGBONE. *(Mockingly)* She wants to know what happened to the porpoise.
MURDOCK. Hungry little shark. Ha, ha, ha.
MRS. HERRINGBONE. Ha, ha, ha.
LORELEI. *(Forcing herself)* Ha, ha, ha.

[Music: THINK LIKE A SHARK]

MURDOCK.
THINK LIKE A SHARK, BE OVER-BEARING
DON'T BE A TROUT, DON'T BE A HERRING
THEY'LL FIND YOUR BITE IS WORSE THAN
    YOUR BARK
WHEN YOU THINK LIKE A SHARK.
MRS. HERRINGBONE.
ACT LIKE A SHARK, SLICE LIKE A SURGEON

DON'T BE A SHRIMP, DON'T BE A STURGEON
YOU'LL HAVE YOUR WAY AND THAT IS A FACT
WHEN A SHARK'S HOW YOU ACT.
    LORELEI.
IF YOU'RE ANXIOUS TO SURVIVE
BECOME A CLEVER THINKER
SPREAD YOUR JAWS AND THEY'LL GET CAUGHT
HOOK, LINE AND SINKER
    ALL.
THINK LIKE A SHARK, ACT LIKE A BOUNDER
DON'T BE A COD, DON'T BE A FLOUNDER
THEY'LL GET YOUR POINT AS QUICK AS A
    WINK
WHEN A SHARK'S HOW YOU THINK.
    MURDOCK.
MOVE LIKE A SHARK, SPAIN TO BERMUDA
SHOW THEM THAT YOU'RE A BARRACUDA
YOU'LL FIND THERE IS SO LITTLE TO PROVE
WHEN A SHARK'S HOW YOU MOVE.
    MRS. HERRINGBONE.
SCHEME LIKE A SHARK, NOT POLLYANNA
SHOW THEM YOUR TEETH, BE A PIRANHA
YOU'LL FIND THEY'LL WANT TO BE ON YOUR
    TEAM
WHEN A SHARK'S HOW YOU SCHEME.
    LORELEI.
IF YOU FIND YOU'RE ALL-AT-SEA
THEN COME OUT OF YOUR CLOISTER
WHEN YOU'RE SLIP'ERY AS AN EEL
THE WORLD'S YOUR OYSTER.

ALL.
TELL THEM A TALE, A FISHY STORY
BE MOBY DICK, BE PREDATORY
THEY SOON WILL FIND YOU HAVE MADE
    YOUR MARK
WHEN YOU THINK LIKE A SHARK
WHEN YOU ACT, MOVE, SCHEME AND THINK
    LIKE A SHARK.

MURDOCK. We allow you to live, Lorelei, because you have a calming influence on the professor. With your help, we intend to extract the knowledge we want.

MRS. HERRINGBONE. However, if you continue to give us trouble, you will — *disappear.*

MURDOCK. *(Low)* Hee, hee, hee.

LORELEI. Gulp. *(ANNOUNCER RETURNS with stringed tin cans. Puts them on floor)*

ANNOUNCER. *(Cupping his hands, speaking into the hollow)* Rrrrring, rrrrring, rrrrring. *(ALL turn to desk)*

MRS. HERRINGBONE. Someone is calling on the secret radio set.

MURDOCK. It could be Countess Frederika. Get the professor.

MRS. HERRINGBONE. At once. *(MRS. HERRINGBONE GOES into the cellar)*

MURDOCK. *(To LORELEI)* And, you—

LORELEI. Me?

MURDOCK. Keep an eye on Adam.

LORELEI. What!

MURDOCK. Don't let him go outside. There's a danger of rust.

LORELEI. *(Pleading)* Couldn't you look after him?

Murdock. *(Menacingly, holds up the lash)* What's it to be? The lash or the shark?

Lorelei. I'll take the tomato can. *(She EXITS LEFT)*

Announcer. *(Into his cupped hands)* Rrrrrring, rrrrrring, rrrrring.

Murdock. *(Out to audience)* That radio message concerns — *(One hand up for emphasis)* The Fog! (With that, he *dashes behind the dressing screen.*

Announcer. *(ANNOUNCER picks up the string of tin cans and rattles them at the mike. ADAM, once again, APPEARS in the hallway from LEFT. CLANG, CLANG, CLANG. As always, it seems confused as to where it wants to go. Its arms straight out, it EXITS RIGHT, in the hallway, only to REAPPEAR almost immediately. ANNOUNCER makes a "sound" to suggest a "ping" from a gun. ADAM becomes a "target" — as if he belonged to some amusement park game) Ping! ... Ping! ... Ping!... (Each time ANNOUNCER says "Ping!" the robot spins to the opposite direction. Each "Ping!" represents a hit.* [Keep this going as long as it proves funny] LORELEI ENTERS LEFT, in the room, sees ADAM)

Lorelei. There you are. Come with me. *(Suddenly, ADAM stops, reacts to the voice. Looks to LORELEI)* Yes, it's me talking to you, you great lump. I don't like this any better than you. But I'm not letting you out of my sight. This way. *(LORELEI turns, EXITS LEFT. Instead of following her, ADAM thumps to the cellar entry, EXITS. As he moves, ANNOUNCER shakes the tin cans. When ADAM is OUT, ANNOUNCER EXITS. Pause)*

Murdock's Voice. *(From behind the screen)* And now, for another appearance by — *The Fog! (He pops INTO VIEW from behind the screen. He wears a black cape with a high collar, black gloves. Over his face is a black hood with two openings for the eyes. Naturally, he looks like an absolute fool. Moves to the desk and, from beneath it, removes a suitcase. He puts it atop the desk and flips it open. From the interior he takes out a hand microphone and a set of headphones. The "radio" is supposedly within the suitcase. CAP'N SCAR ENTERS radio studio, stands at microphone. The actor is dressed like the classic story pirate — boots, sash, colorful blouse, bandana on his head or a wide-brimmed hat, earring. One hand is a hook, one eye is covered with an eye patch. Optional stuffed parrot sits on his shoulder. Large scar running down one cheek. As MURDOCK goes about his business, he mumbles rather madly)*

MURDOCK. No one will stand in the way of my plans … ha, ha, ha. I'm too clever for them. Too clever for them all. Hee, hee, hee. I, The Fog, will use them for my purposes, and when I am through, I will feed them to the shark. Hee, hee, hee. *(Deadly serious, he stops mumbling. Puts headset to one ear, grabs the hand mike. His voice is dark and mysterious)* This is The Fog speaking. Come in, come in, whoever you are.

CAP'N SCAR. That you, Fog?

MURDOCK. This is The Fog speaking.

CAP'N SCAR. Huh?

MURDOCK. *(Furious)* I said, "This is The Fog speaking!"

CAP'N SCAR. Cap'n Scar here.

MURDOCK. What do you want?

CAP'N SCAR. I have some "merchandise" to deliver. Is it safe?

MURDOCK. I'm not certain I want any more "merchandise." I have bigger fish to fry.

CAP'N SCAR. *(Threatening tone)* Don't pull any tricks, Frog.

MURDOCK. *Fog!*

CAP'N SCAR. Tricks wouldn't be healthy.

MURDOCK. *(Enraged)* Don't threaten me, you water-logged barracuda. No one threatens The Fog!

CAP'N SCAR. We have a business arrangement, Fog. *(Threatening tone)* "Gentlemen" don't break business arrangements. It could be "unwise" — if you get my meaning.

MURDOCK. *(Reluctant)* Very well. Make your delivery.

CAP'N SCAR. That's better.

MURDOCK. You know the setup. The Fog is signing off. Over and out. *(CAP'N SCAR EXITS. MURDOCK puts headphones and microphone back into the suitcase. SOUND OF REVERBERATING GONG. Immediately, MRS. HERRING-BONE APPEARS from the cellar and LORELEI APPEARS from LEFT)*

MRS. HERRINGBONE. What was that?

LORELEI. What was that?

MURDOCK. What was that?

ALL. The doorbell.

MRS. HERRINGBONE. Nobody comes to Nightmare Castle.

LORELEI. It's too remote.

MURDOCK. Countess Frederika wouldn't dare risk it. Where's the professor?

MRS. HERRINGBONE. I left him below. He was proving difficult. *(Again, the SOUND OF REVERBERATING GONG)* There it is again.

LORELEI. What are you going to do?

MURDOCK. There's nothing to fear, as long as we keep our wits. *(Puts suitcase beneath desk)*

MRS. HERRINGBONE. Could it be Cap'n Scar?

MURDOCK. No. I just spoke with him on the secret radio. It must be our one neighbor. The pest.

MRS. HERRINGBONE. Nyoka Sterling?

MURDOCK. Who else? Always popping in and out with her miserable home cooking.

LORELEI. I like her home cooking. Especially the chocolate chips.

MURDOCK. *Shut up!*

LORELEI. Sorry.

MRS. HERRINGBONE. Nyoka Sterling never strikes the gong. If she wants to come in, she comes in.

MURDOCK. One day she'll come in and see too much. And then—

ALL. *(Dramatic)* The shark.

BETTY'S VOICE. *(OFFSTAGE; from hallway)* Hello, hello. Anybody home?

MRS. HERRINGBONE. That's not Nyoka Sterling.

LORELEI. Who can it be?

MRS. HERRINGBONE. Whoever she is, she's not wanted here. We must get rid of her.

MURDOCK. Drat! *(He darts behind the dressing screen. As he does so, BETTY COMES INTO VIEW. Both LORELEI and MRS. HERRINGBONE freeze. A visitor at Nightmare Castle?)*

BETTY. *(Sees them)* I wasn't sure anyone was here. We did strike the gong. *(Over their shock, MRS. HERRING-BONE and LORELEI relax a bit)*

MRS. HERRINGBONE. Obviously, there's been some

mistake. We never have visitors.

LORELEI. In the daytime.

MRS. HERRINGBONE. *(Snaps)* Be still, you foolish girl.

LORELEI. Sorry.

BETTY. I'm not a visitor. I'm a relative. Betty Parker.

MRS. HERRINGBONE. Relative?

LORELEI. What kind of relative?

BETTY. I'm Professor Murdock's niece.

OTHERS. *(Stunned)* Niece!

BETTY. Yes, niece. *(Flat)* It's the female form of nephew. *(Steps into room)* Uncle Philo wrote and asked to see me.

MRS. HERRINGBONE. He did?

BETTY. I doubt if he'll recognize me. Last time I saw him I was little more than an infant. *(MRS. HAR-RINGBONE and LORELEI exchange a nervous glance)* Is something wrong?

MRS. HERRINGBONE. The road has been washed out for some time. How did you manage to get here?

BETTY. Flew.

LORELEI. You've got the flu?

BETTY. We came in a plane. We would have been here sooner, only we had an accident.

LORELEI. What kind of accident?

BETTY. We crashed.

MRS. HERRINGBONE. And who is "we?"

BETTY. My best friend. *(Gestures UPSTAGE)* Dan Daredevil. *(MRS. HERRINGBONE is aghast. She recognizes the name)*

MRS. HERRINGBONE. Dan Daredevil? America's number one hero?

Betty. The same. *(Calls to hallway)* Need any help, Dan?

Dan's Voice. *(OFFSTAGE; from hallway)* I can manage. *(Pause for impact, and then DAN DAREDEVIL MAKES HIS ENTRANCE. He hobbles with the aid of a crutch. One arm is in a sling. He stops, smiles)*

Dan. *(Boyishly)* Hi, one and all. *(ABOUT DAN'S COSTUME: Now that he's out of the plane, we can get a good look. He wears an aviator's cap with the goggles pushed back. [At an opportune moment, actor can remove cap and goggles if he wishes] A leather jacket with flight wings painted on one side, scarf. Leather belt, gloves. His trousers are jodhpurs. Boots that come almost to his knees)*

Mrs. Herringbone. I am Mrs. Herringbone, the housekeeper. *(Nods to LORELEI)* This is the hired girl, Lorelei.

Lorelei. Pleased to make your acquaintance, likewise. *(She curtsies)*

Mrs. Herringbone. Pay the girl no mind. She means well. Unfortunately, she's quite stupid.

Dan. *(Hobbles into room)* Maybe if I sat down, I'd be able to take care of this leg.

Mrs. Herringbone. *(Indicates sofa)* Please. *(DAN hobbles to sofa, sits)*

Dan. I can't do this operation unless I'm sitting down. It doesn't work if I'm standing up. That's why I have to sit down.

Mrs. Herringbone. I understand.

Dan. *(DAN hands the crutch to BETTY)* I always fly with a crutch. In case of emergencies. *(With great effort, a grimace on his face, he straightens out his leg)* That's better.

LORELEI. What was the matter with your leg?

DAN. Broken. And now — the arm. *(He removes the sling, passes it to BETTY. The lower arm dangles from the elbow like a twig in the breeze. With great effort, another grimace, DAN straightens out the arm)* That's better. The broken bones are mended in place.

LORELEI. Wow! I've never seen anything like that. Wow!

DAN. It's nothing. A trick I learned in India when I was working for the Internal Revenue Service. *(While attention is diverted, MURDOCK, who has heard everything, steps from behind the screen. He's no longer wearing The Fog drag. He EXITS LEFT in hallway, so he can reappear shortly)*

MRS. HERRINGBONE. Amazzzzzing. *(DAN gives her a cold eye)*

DAN. Yes, I suppose you could say that.

MRS. HERRINGBONE. *(To LORELEI)* You say your uncle wrote to you?

BETTY. I have the letter right here. *(She doesn't know what to do with the crutch and sling)*

LORELEI. I'll take those.

BETTY. Thanks. *(LORELEI takes crutch and sling, EXITS LEFT. BETTY takes envelope from some pocket)*

MURDOCK'S VOICE. *(OFFSTAGE; from hallway)* Who was at the door, Mrs. Herringbone?

MRS. HERRINGBONE. *(Calls UPSTAGE)* A Miss Betty Parker. *(ANNOUNCER ENTERS, stands in front of radio studio mike. MURDOCK pretends to be a "loving uncle." Arms wide for an embrace, he ENTERS the main room. DAN stands)*

MURDOCK. Betty! My dear niece. My dear girl. It's been

so long. *(As MURDOCK moves CENTER, Woof threatens)*

ANNOUNCER. *Grrrrr! Grrrrr! Grrrrr! (*Business: *The unseen dog is attempting to "attack" MURDOCK, snarling, growling)*

MURDOCK. Back! Back! Betty, is this your dog!?

ANNOUNCER. *Grrrrr! Grrrrr! Grrrrr!*

MRS. HERRINGBONE. It's attacking Professor Murdock!

MURDOCK. Get away, get away, dog!

ANNOUNCER. *Grrrrr! Grrrrr! Grrrrr!*

BETTY. Dan, do something.

MURDOCK. He's got my leg. Let go! Let go!

ANNOUNCER. *Grrrrr! Grrrrr! Grrrrr!*

DAN. Woof! *(MURDOCK, frantic, attempts to shake loose the dog. Kicks his leg, pulls at his trouser leg, hops about)*

ANNOUNCER. *Grrrrr! Grrrrr! Grrrrr!*

DAN. *(Loud command)* That's enough, Woof!

ANNOUNCER. *(Gently)* Woof, woof, woof. *(DAN snaps his fingers and, supposedly, Woof ambles to him)*

DAN. *(Patting Woof)* Good boy, good boy. *(With his hands held like paws, ANNOUNCER "pants")*

BETTY. I can't imagine what got into Woof. He's usually such a gentle dog.

ANNOUNCER. *(Softly)* Woof.

MURDOCK. *(Notices envelope in BETTY'S hand)* Is that my letter?

BETTY. Yes, it is, Uncle.

MURDOCK. May I see it, dear?

BETTY. Certainly. *(She hands the envelope to MURDOCK, who removes the letter)*

DAN. I am terribly sorry about Woof, Professor Murdock.

MURDOCK. Let's hear no more about the dog. Strange surroundings often upset animals.

DAN. You're very understanding, Professor.

MURDOCK. You are, uh — ?

BETTY. This is Dan Daredevil.

MURDOCK. Daredevil?

MRS. HERRINGBONE. *(Pointedly)* You've heard of Dan Daredevil, Professor. America's number one hero. He's always in the newspapers for one good deed or another. Fights crime.

DAN. *(Chest out)* "The whole purpose of my life is watching out for the little guy."

MURDOCK. How commendable. *(To BETTY)* Sit down, my dear. Sit down. *(BETTY sits by desk)* You, too, Mr. Daredevil.

DAN. Thank you, Professor. *(DAN sits, pats Woof)*

ANNOUNCER. *(Softly)* Woof. *(ANNOUNCER EXITS)*

MURDOCK. *(The letter)* "Dear Niece Betty, no doubt you'll be surprised to hear from your old Uncle Philo after all these years... I am in great danger... need help... you're my only living relative... come at once..." *(Returns letter to envelope)* I remember writing this, but I can't imagine what I was referring to.

DAN. You're not in danger?

MURDOCK. Danger? Pshaw. *(Returns envelope to BETTY)*

MRS. HERRINGBONE. The Professor often has lapses. He's been known to do odd things at odd times. Like writing that letter.

BETTY. Uncle Philo, you never wrote to me before.

DAN. The letter sounded so urgent.

MURDOCK. I am sorry if I've inconvenienced you both. I assure you I am quite all right. Let's look on the bright side. *(Steps to BETTY)* After all this time we finally meet again.

BETTY. We could have met before this, Uncle Philo. But you're such a recluse. You never wanted people to visit.

MRS. HERRINGBONE. We don't want to detain you. I'm sure you want to be on your way.

DAN. What?

BETTY. We just got here.

DAN. Not only that — the plane needs repair.

NYOKA'S VOICE. *(OFFSTAGE; from hallway)* Yoo-hoo. Yoo-hoo.

MURDOCK. Drat.

DAN. Something wrong, Professor?

MURDOCK. A pesty neighbor. Always dropping in when she's not wanted.

MRS. HERRINGBONE. Nyoka Sterling. *(ALL look UP-STAGE. A moment's pause, and then NYOKA ENTERS. She's a fussy, gushy, middle-aged type. Tweeds. Carries a basket covered with a checkered napkin)*

NYOKA. I was baking gingerbread men and I thought to myself, I'll bet Nightmare Castle would love a few. *(Sees DAN and BETTY)* Oh, company?

MURDOCK. My niece Betty.

BETTY. Hello. *(Indicates)* My lifelong friend — Dan Daredevil.

NYOKA. *(Fascinated)* Not *the* Dan Daredevil.

DAN. *(Stands, indicates)* And my wonder dog, Woof.

NYOKA. *(Meaning the dog)* Isn't he sweet? *(Holds up the basket to DAN)* Gingerbread man?

MURDOCK. Prepare rooms for our guests, Mrs. Herringbone.

MRS. HERRINGBONE. *(Alarmed)* You mean — they're staying?

MURDOCK. *(With hidden meaning)* I want their visit to be "memorable."

BETTY. You really want us to stay, Uncle Philo?

MURDOCK. I do, indeed. *(As MUSIC STARTS, LORELEI ENTERS)*

[Music: MAKE YOURSELF AT HOME, MY DEAR]

MURDOCK, MRS. HERRINGBONE, NYOKA, LORELEI.
MAKE YOURSELF AT HOME, MY DEAR, SO GLAD
   YOU'RE HERE TODAY.
WE WELCOME YOU WITH OPEN ARMS AND HOPE
   THAT YOU WILL STAY.
REST ASSURED THAT YOU HAVE FOUND A PLACE
   TO HANG YOUR HAT.
MAKE YOURSELF AT HOME AS WE ROLL OUT THE
   WELCOME MAT.
MRS. HERRINGBONE.
YOU'LL LOVE THE SOUND OF CRASHING WAVES
   AND THUNDER IN THE NIGHT
AND WHEN YOU WATCH THE LIGHTNING FLASH
   IT'S SUCH A PLEASANT SIGHT.
MURDOCK.
ALTHOUGH WE KNOW YOU'VE JUST ARRIVED

YOU MUSTN'T BE A STRANGER
AND LET US REASSURE YOU THAT THERE'S NOT
  THE SLIGHTEST DANGER.
Lorelei.
YOU'LL HEAR THE SOUND OF ORGAN TUNES
  A'FLOATING THROUGH THE AIR
AND LEARN TO LOVE THE CLANKING CHAINS
  BOTH UP AND DOWN THE STAIR.
Nyoka.
AND THOUGH THE RUMORS FLY ABOUT, YOU
  MUST REMAIN UNDAUNTED
IT'S MERELY IDLE GOSSIP THAT THE CASTLE'S
  REALLY HAUNTED.
Murdock, Mrs. Herringbone, Nyoka, Lorelei.
MAKE YOURSELF AT HOME, MY DEAR, SO GLAD
  YOU'RE HERE TODAY.
WE WELCOME YOU WITH OPEN ARMS AND HOPE
  THAT YOU WILL STAY.
REST ASSURED THAT YOU HAVE FOUND A PLACE
  TO HANG YOUR HAT.
MAKE YOURSELF AT HOME AS WE ROLL OUT
  THE WELCOME MAT.
Mrs. Herringbone.
YOU'LL SELDOM HEAR A SCREAM AT NIGHT, BUT
  THERE COULD BE SOME MOANS
ALONG WITH KNOCKS, AND RAPS, AND THUMPS
  AND, NOW AND THEN, SOME GROANS.
Murdock.
THOUGH STORIES SEEM TO FLY ABOUT AND
  SOUND A BIT DRAMATIC
THERE'S NO DEMENTED RELATIVE WHO'S HID-

DEN IN THE ATTIC.

Lorelei.

OH, NOW AND THEN THE HINGES CREAK OR YOU MIGHT HEAR A THUD

AND SOMETIMES GHOSTLY RATTLES CAUSE A CURDLING OF THE BLOOD.

Nyoka.

WE'RE GLAD YOU MADE YOUR WAY TO US, IT MUST HAVE BEEN A HASSLE

BUT HERE YOU ARE, THE BOTH OF YOU, SO SAFE AT NIGHTMARE CASTLE.

Murdock, Mrs. Herringbone, Nyoka, Lorelei.

MAKE YOURSELF AT HOME, MY DEAR, SO GLAD YOU'RE HERE TODAY.

Dan & Betty.

YOU'VE WELCOMED US WITH OPEN ARMS, WE KNOW THAT WE WILL STAY.

REST ASSURED THAT WE HAVE FOUND A PLACE TO HANG OUR HAT.

WE'LL MAKE OURSELVES AT HOME AS YOU ROLL OUT THE WELCOME MAT.

All.

(WE'LL) MAKE (OURSELVES/YOURSELF) AT HOME AS (YOU/WE) ROLL OUT THE WELCOME MAT.

Mrs. Herringbone. *(To LORELEI)* The rooms in the west tower are always ready for "visitors." Lorelei, show the Professor's guests to their quarters.

Lorelei. Yes, ma'am. *(LORELEI moves to hallway)* This way. *(BETTY and DAN move to follow)*

Murdock. We'll have a chat over dinner. It's liver.

BETTY. That'll be nice, Uncle Philo.

DAN. Come on, Woof. *(LORELEI, BETTY and DAN are OUT LEFT)*

NYOKA. Imagine! Dan Daredevil here at Nightmare Castle.

MURDOCK. Please don't call my home Nightmare Castle. It offends me.

NYOKA. I apologize. I keep forgetting. *(Holds up basket)* I'll put the cookies on the kitchen table. *(She quickly moves into hallway, LEFT)* Dan Daredevil! Imagine. *(She's OUT)*

MURDOCK. Wretched woman.

MRS. HERRINGBONE. How could the Professor have smuggled out a letter?

MURDOCK. He must have given it to the robot. Adam is extremely clever. I *must* learn its secret. *I must! (BETTY'S real UNCLE PHILO stumbles IN from cellar. He looks as if he's been shipwrecked for years. No shoes, his trousers are torn. His shirt is ragged. He has a dirty gray beard almost to the waist. Dishevelled hair. He has shackles on his wrists and his mind is almost gone)*

PHILO. *(To MURDOCK)* Never!

MRS. HERRINGBONE. The Professor!

MURDOCK. I'll fix him! *(Gets whip)*

PHILO. I heard everything! I was listening at the door. My niece is here.

MRS. HERRINGBONE. You're imagining things again, Professor. Hearing noises again. Get below and chain yourself to the wall.

PHILO. I won't give you the information you need. Never, never!

MURDOCK. We'll see about that.

PHILO. *(Bravely)* You can beat me! You can starve me! You can humiliate me! You can torture me! But you won't break my will to resist!

MURDOCK. *Get below! (Cracks the whip)*

PHILO. *(Meekly)* Whatever you say. *(Like a frightened mouse, PHILO scurries BACK INTO the cellar. ANNOUNCER ENTERS, stands at mike with script. MURDOCK and MRS. HERRINGBONE FOLLOW after PHILO. LIGHTS FADE on main room)*

ANNOUNCER. Yes, radio fans, Dan and Betty have really gotten themselves into a jam this time. Little do they realize the man who says he is Professor Murdock is actually the arch-criminal known as The Fog. What is the "merchandise" the weird Cap'n Scar is planning to deliver? And who is Countess Frederika? *(Change in inflection)* Keep pencil and paper ready for the instructions on how to get your personal Dan Daredevil invisibility ring and secret decoder. *(Building excitement)* And now, back to Nightmare Castle. The sea mist is rolling in and it's almost dinnertime. They're having liver. Outside the house is all dark. No sound except for the mournful cry of a distant foghorn. *(ANNOUNCER makes sound of foghorn, EXITS. MRS. HERRINGBONE APPEARS "on the cliff." In one hand she holds a lantern [or flashlight]. She is signalling to a boat in the water. At the same time, LORELEI COMES DOWN the stairs. BETTY and DAN are behind her. LIGHTS DIM UP. LORELEI talks fast, making an impulsive confession)*

LORELEI. I'm so glad you're here. Honest, I am. I only agreed to help them because they said if I didn't I'd regret it. I'm a coward.

BETTY. What are you talking about? *(DAN sees something out the window)*

DAN. That's interesting.

BETTY. What?

DAN. Through the window. *(Points to window)* Out there in the dark. *(DAN moves to window. BETTY stands over the trapdoor)*

BETTY. You won't be able to see anything. The fog.

LORELEI. The Fog? Don't say that, don't say that. If you only knew—

DAN. Somebody is signalling with a light. *(What DAN supposedly sees is the lantern glow. The laugh comes from the fact DAN is looking OFF LEFT while MRS. HERRINGBONE is EXTREME DOWN RIGHT, "on the cliff")*

BETTY. *(Looks to window)* Who, I wonder?

DAN. Why, I wonder?

LORELEI. Could be any one of them. They're all wicked.

BETTY. Who's wicked? *(MRS. HERRINGBONE snaps off light, EXITS)*

DAN. There goes the light.

LORELEI. *(Babbling)* He says he's your uncle, but he's not. He's The Fog and Mrs. Herringbone helps him and they've locked up your real uncle and there's a robot and a man who has a hook for a hand ... *(BETTY and DAN exchange a look. BETTY taps her forehead to indicate that LORELEI is demented)* I saw that. You think I'm crazy.

BETTY. No, no, no.

DAN. You're the nervous type, that's all.

LORELEI. You don't believe me. You don't believe anything I'm saying. They only let me live because I'm a calming influence on the Professor. *(Suddenly, her voice drops. To BETTY—)* What would you say if I told you you're standing over a shark?

BETTY. Oops. *(She jumps back)*

LORELEI. I try to run away, but they always catch me. *(She starts to sob, moves to sofa. Sits)* I told them I was going to the police, but they said they'd feed me to the shark. Sharks and robots, oh, oh. *(She bawls. BETTY moves to sofa, sits beside LORELEI, puts a comforting arm across her shoulder)*

BETTY. There, there. You are in a bad way. *(DAN moves to UPSTAGE side of rug)*

LORELEI. I've got an idea. Why don't we repair the plane. We can all fly out of here?

BETTY. I'm afraid there's only room for two. You'd have to sit on Dan's lap.

LORELEI. I wouldn't mind. *(By now, DAN has lifted the rug and the "trapdoor." Looks below)*

DAN. What do you know!

BETTY. What?

DAN. *There is a shark under the rug.*

BETTY. *(Jumps up)* Are you trying to be funny?

DAN. See for yourself. *(BETTY moves to look)*

LORELEI. I better see what the tomato can's up to. I don't want any more trouble. *(Stifling a sob, LORELEI EXITS LEFT. Neither DAN nor BETTY notice her departure. Their interest is strictly on what's "below." BETTY looks, gives a little scream)*

DAN. Maybe that maid isn't so crazy. *(Closes "trapdoor," drops rug. Stands)*

BETTY. I knew Uncle Philo was into some weird things. It was a family scandal. But I never suspected his weird was this weird.

DAN. It's weird, all right. I'll tell you something else, Betty.

BETTY. What, Dan?

DAN. I recognized Mrs. Herringbone. And she recognized I recognized her.

BETTY. So?

DAN. I once broke up a gang of dangerous kidnappers, and they were headed by—

BETTY. Mrs. Herringbone!?

DAN. Yes. Mrs. Herringbone. Lorelei, you said something about The Fog. *(Looks about)* Where is she?

BETTY. *(Looks)* You can't pay attention to anything she says, Dan. She's got a brain like a scrambled egg.

DAN. That shark is no scrambled egg, and The Fog is no weather report. He's an unscrupulous villain. A criminal mastermind.

BETTY. *(Gasping)* Criminal mastermind?

DAN. A grotesquely-clad scoundrel! A masked devil. He's brilliant.

BETTY. You think he's involved with Mrs. Herringbone?

DAN. I think this is a job for the Dan Daredevil invisibility ring. *(Looks about)* I'll go behind that screen. Woof, you stay here with Betty. *(BETTY turns her head to one side and gives a "Woof." DAN ducks behind the screen)*

DAN'S VOICE. I never allow anyone to see how the invisibility ring works. Not even you, Betty. Sorry.

BETTY. I understand, Dan.

DAN'S VOICE. I'm removing my glove and I'm giving the ring a special twist I learned in the mountains of Tibet. When I reappear, you will hear my voice, Betty. But I will be — *invisible!*

BETTY. *(Impressed)* Ready when you are, Dan.

DAN'S VOICE. Here I come, Betty. *(Pause. DAN pops out from behind the screen. Strikes a Superman pose, fists on hips, head high)*

DAN. I'm over here, Betty. I can see you, but you can't see me. Dan Daredevil, invisible crime fighter. *(Pause. BETTY looks blankly into audience, and then back to DAN)*

BETTY. But I can see you, Dan.

DAN. *(Uneasy)* You can?

BETTY. *(Somewhat embarrassed)* Uh-huh.

DAN. *(Fools with the ring)* Something must be wrong with the ring. Happens every now and then. *(Attempts to get ring from his finger)* I'll have to take it back to Tibet for repairs. *(Continues to tug at the ring, moving DOWNSTAGE)* It's a good thing I came along with you, Betty. That shark is an ill omen. I smell dirty work at Nightmare Castle, and that means — *Dan Daredevil to the rescue!*

[Music: THE THRILL OF IT ALL]

DAN.
OH, THE THRILL OF IT ALL.
OH, THE THRILL OF IT ALL.
BREATH-TAKING CHASES ON RUNAWAY TRAINS
(ADAM enters and pursues BETTY, who tries to flee)
DANGER FALLS INTO MY LAP.
GOTTA BE CAREFUL OR I COULD WALK INTO
  A TRAP.

IT'S EXCITING! AND
FIRST I'M SAVING A LIFE
(BETTY calls "Help")
THEN I'M DODGING A KNIFE.
(BETTY calls "Help!" again)
TRAPPED IN A DUNGEON WITH POISONOUS
   SNAKES
(ADAM picks up BETTY and starts to exit)
THERE I AM CHAINED TO THE WALL
OH, THE THRILL OF IT ALL!
(As BETTY exits she screams "Dan, Dan!")
IT'S EXCITING WHEN I'M
THERE TO STOP EV'RY CRIME.
HAIR-RAISING RESCUES AND SINISTER SCHEMES
SOMETIMES A VERY CLOSE SHAVE
KIDNAPPERS TIE ME INSIDE OF AN UNDER-
   GROUND CAVE
FULL OF DYNAMITE!
FIRST I'M PULLED AND I'M DRAGGED
(CAP'N SCAR enters and menaces DAN with his hook)
THEN I'M BOUND AND I'M GAGGED.
RIGHT OUT OF NOWHERE A ROBOT APPEARS
LOOKS LIKE HE'S SEVEN FEET TALL
OH!
*(DAN punches CAP'N SCAR and he is knocked to the floor,
"unconscious")*
THE THRILL OF IT ALL!
LIKE THOSE HEROES IN BOOKS
I IMPRISON THE CROOKS.
SPINE-TINGLING INTRIGUE AND NARROW ES-
   CAPES

JUST BY THE SKIN OF MY TEETH.
THEN IN THE OCEAN I'M TRAPPED NINETY
  FATHOMS BENEATH
IN A SUBMARINE!
NOW MY PARACHUTE STRAP
(MURDOCK, as "THE FOG," creeps in and menaces DAN)
IS BEGINNING TO SNAP.
HAVING A FIST-FIGHT ON TOP OF A CLIFF
LOOKS LIKE I'M GOING TO FALL
OH!
(DAN punches him out. "THE FOG" drops to the floor)
THE THRILL OF IT ALL!
OH, THE THRILL OF A CHASE.
(ADAM enters and clunks towards DAN)
DEATH IS RIGHT IN MY FACE
(ADAM wraps his arms around DAN'S body)
ENEMY SPIES WANT TO CONQUER THE WORLD
SMASHING THEIR PLOT IS MY THING.
THEN IF I'M CORNERED, WITH ONE LITTLE
  TWIST OF MY RING
I'M INVISIBLE!
(DAN breaks hold and ADAM spins around)
OH, THE THRILL OF IT ALL!
*(CAP'N SCAR and MURDOCK "regain consciousness," rise, get
props and advance on DAN)*
OH, THE THRILL OF IT ALL!
TRAPPED IN A FIRE ON THE FIFTIETH FLOOR
LOOKS LIKE ANOTHER CLOSE CALL.
OH, THE THRILL OF IT
EACH THRILLING CHILL AND SPILL OF IT
(SCAR, MURDOCK and ADAM are poised to strike)

OH!
(SCAR, MURDOCK, ADAM and DAN all freeze in pose)
    ANNOUNCER. *(Interrupting, at studio mike. DAREDEVIL-ETTES in)* It looks like curtains for Dan Daredevil! Will he escape The Fog? *(MUSICAL CHORD)* Cap'n Scar? *(CHORD)* Adam the Robot? *(CHORD)* And what has happened to pretty Betty Parker? *(CHORD)* Don't miss the next thrilling installment of The Amazzzzzing Adventures of Dan Daredevil. Coming to you right after intermission.
    DAREDEVILETTES. *(Singing)*
THE THRILL OF IT ALL!

BLACKOUT

END OF ACT I

ACT II

ANNOUNCER and DAREDEVILETTES are in the radio studio. DIM LIGHT on Nightmare Castle.

DAREDEVILETTES. *(Echoing)* Dan Daredevil, Dan Daredevil, Dan Daredevil...

ANNOUNCER. *(Script in hand, into mike)* Well, gang, I wish I could give you a clearer picture of what's been happening to Dan Daredevil and pretty Betty Parker at Nightmare Castle and, perhaps I can. But first, another word from our sponsor — Crunchy Chews. *(He steps aside and the DAREDEVILETTES take the mike)*

[Music: CRUNCHY CHEWS]

DAREDEVILETTES.
CRUNCHY CHEWY!
CHEWY CRUNCHY!
CRUNCHY CHEWY!
CHEWY CRUNCHY!
CRUNCHY CHEWY!
CHEWY CRUNCHY!
CRUNCHY CHEWS!
OH, DAN AND WOOF, THE WONDER DOG, HAVE
   GOT A HUNCH.
THEY KNOW YOU'LL LOVE THE DOG FOOD WITH
   A LOT OF PUNCH.

THEY EAT IT EV'RY DAY AT BREAKFAST-TIME
  AND LUNCH.
YOU'LL LOVE CRUNCHY CHEWS A DOG-GONE
  BUNCH!
ANNOUNCER.
WOOF!
(DAREDEVILETTES step back. ANNOUNCER takes the mike)
Thank you, Daredevilettes. And for all you fans out there
who already have the Dan Daredevil secret decoder, stay
tuned for an important message. But first — *(The script)*
Yes, indeed, radio fans, things are getting confused at
Nightmare Castle. This much we know! Professor Philo
Murdock, world-famous scientist and recluse, is being
held prisoner by the master criminal known only as The
Fog. *(DAREDEVILETTES gasp)* And The Fog is in league
with the notorious Mrs. Herringbone. *(Another gasp)* And
the appearance of the mysterious person calling himself
Cap'n Scar can only mean more trouble for Dan. *(Another
gasp)* All has not gone well at Nightmare Castle. Thrills
ahead as we experience *Amazzzzzing* Adventures of —
  ALL. *(ECHOING and REVERBERATING)* Dan Daredevil, Dan Daredevil, Dan Daredevil... *(LIGHTS FADE on
radio studio. DAREDEVILETTES EXIT. ANNOUNCER cups
his hands, speaks into the hollow to simulate the ring of the
secret radio)*
  ANNOUNCER. Rrrrrring, Rrrrrring, Rrrrrring. *(LIGHTS
UP at Nightmare Castle)*
  MURDOCK'S VOICE. *(OFFSTAGE; from cellar)* Drat!
*(MURDOCK ENTERS, goes to desk to get the radio. He's dressed
as "THE FOG." Same business as in ACT I. Puts suitcase on desk
top, gets headphones, hand mike. As he does this business, he mum-*

bles his irritation)

MURDOCK. Cap'n Scar would show up just in time to muddy the waters ... I'll soon deal with him ... and Dan Daredevil, too ... nothing is going to mess up this deal ... too much is at stake ... I'm surrounded by incompetence ... If you want anything done right, you have to do it yourself ... *(We catch a fleeting glimpse of BETTY as she RUNS BY in the hallway, nervously looking over her shoulder. In a few seconds, ADAM CLANGS after her, arms out-stretched)* I'm as good a scientist as Philo Murdock any day ... *(COUNTESS FREDERICKA ENTERS radio studio and stands at the microphone. A cool, elegant femme fatale. Gorgeously dressed, in the most expensive style [a backless, slinky evening gown will also work nicely]. Flashing jewelry. Perfect coiffure. Beneath her sophistication and beauty — pure evil. Foreign intrigue accent. MURDOCK speaks with a dark, mysterious voice)* This is The Fog speaking.

FREDERIKA. Countess Frederika.

MURDOCK. I suspected it was you, Countess.

FREDERIKA. You're wasting too much valuable time. Have you gotten the required information from Professor Murdock?

MURDOCK. We may not need him. I'm working with my own observations and calculations.

FREDERIKA. Don't be a fool, Fog. Only Philo Murdock has the information I require. *An army of robots, marching to conquer the world!*

MURDOCK. Adam needs more work.

FREDERIKA. That's why we need the Professor, you idiot. *Nothing* must go wrong. You understand?

MURDOCK. Uh, er—

FREDERIKA. *(Suspicious)* Something has gone wrong?

MURDOCK. Dan Daredevil is here.

FREDERIKA. Dan Daredevil! *(Calms)* How did that happen?

MURDOCK. It's a long story.

FREDERIKA. I see you've managed to bungle things as usual. The unnamed foreign powers I represent will not be pleased. I am coming to Nightmare Castle. *(She EXITS)*

MURDOCK. No, no. Don't do that. I can handle things. *(Pause)* Countess? Countess Frederika? *(Realizes she's gone)* Drat.

MRS. HERRINGBONE. *(ENTERING from hallway)* What about Dan Daredevil?

MURDOCK. Leave him to me. Put away the radio. *(MURDOCK moves behind screen. MRS. HERRINGBONE puts the radio away. Dialogue through this business)*

MRS. HERRINGBONE. He recognized me.

MURDOCK'S VOICE. Say you have a twin sister.

MRS. HERRINGBONE. *(Scoffs)* Twin sister.

MURDOCK'S VOICE. We've got something else to worry about.

MRS. HERRINGBONE. What?

MURDOCK'S VOICE. Countess Frederika is coming here. She's unhappy with our progress. I'm a brilliant man, but Countess Frederika makes me feel like a Boy Scout.

MRS. HERRINGBONE. *(Worried)* she doesn't know about Cap'n Scar and our little side racket.

MURDOCK'S VOICE. No need to remind me.

MRS. HERRINGBONE. She'll be furious.

MURDOCK'S VOICE. Say nothing to her. You were supposed to warn Capn' Scar away.

MRS. HERRINGBONE. I signalled a warning, but he ignored it. What are we going to do?

MURDOCK. *(Appearing from behind the screen. Out of THE FOG costume)* We're going to pay another visit on the Professor. *(Quick, he moves to cellar and OUT. MRS. HERRINGBONE FOLLOWS. BETTY runs INTO the room from hallway, exhausted. Moves to sofa, sits. Her breathing is audible, coming in tiny gasps. NYOKA ENTERS LEFT. She has the basket)*

NYOKA. Is anything wrong, Miss Parker?

BETTY. Oh!

NYOKA. Forgive me. I didn't mean to frighten you.

BETTY. You didn't frighten me. It was a mechanical man. I was chased by a robot.

NYOKA. Adam. It's one of your uncle's experiments. Clever, don't you think?

BETTY. A thing like that needs a license.

DAN. *(Bouncing IN from hallway, all gusto and bravado)* I don't know where he went, but I'll track him down.

BETTY. Who?

DAN. The pirate.

BETTY & NYOKA. Pirate?

DAN. And The Fog. I fought them off. The robot, too.

BETTY. The robot's almost human.

NYOKA. I have no idea what you're talking about, Dan. But, my, you lead an exciting life.

BETTY. *(Flirting look to DAN)* Dan Daredevil has a lot to worry about. And I worry a lot about Dan Daredevil.

Nyoka. I never worry.

Betty. Never?

Nyoka. If I'm troubled, I go into the kitchen —and bake.

Dan & Betty. Bake?

[Music: A BASKET OF GOODIES]

Nyoka.

IF THE PROBLEMS OF LIFE ARE DEPRESSING

AND YOU'RE HAVING A MIS'RABLE DAY

GO INTO YOUR KITCHEN AND TURN ON YOUR
    OVEN

AND BAKE ALL YOUR WORRIES AWAY.

CHOC'LATE CHIP COOKIES OR CHEESECAKE OR
    BOSTON CREAM PIE,

STIR UP A WONDERFUL BASKET OF GOODIES
    TO TRY.

BLACKBERRY COBBLER OR CUPCAKES OR CO-
COANUT CRUNCH

FIX UP A MARVELOUS BASKET OF GOODIES TO
    MUNCH.

WHEN LIFE IS UPSETTING AND EV'RYTHING
    SWEET HAS TURNED SOUR

GET OUT THE SUGAR, THE BUTTER, THE EGGS
    AND THE FLOUR.

STRAWBERRY SHORTCAKE IS ALWAYS A POP-
ULAR TREAT

BAKE UP A FABULOUS BASKET OF GOODIES TO
    EAT.

Betty.
SERVE UP A CRUMB-CAKE AND DON'T LET A
  CRUMB GO TO WASTE
STIR UP A WONDERFUL BASKET OF GOODIES TO
  TASTE.
Dan.
WHIP UP SOME BROWNIES OR MAYBE A DATE
  BAR, OR TWO,
FIX UP A MARVELOUS BASKET OF GOODIES TO
  CHEW.
Nyoka.
IF TROUBLES APPEAR, MAY I OFFER THIS BIT OF
  ADVICE?
GET OUT VANILLA AND WALNUTS, THE SALT
  AND THE SPICE.
All.
PICK OUT A RECIPE LUSCIOUS AND TEMPTINGLY
  SWEET
BAKE UP A WONDERFUL, MARVELOUS, FABULOUS
BASKET OF GOODIES TO EAT!

Nyoka. I must be running along. *Au revoir. (NYOKA
EXITS into hallway, OUT)*

Betty. Curious neighbor.

Dan. I don't think her prescription will work for me.
Not in my line of work.

Betty. Never mind about her. *(Excitedly)* What's going
on at Nightmare Castle?

Dan. *(Steps to her)* Plenty. *(Displays odd-looking wristwatch)* I picked up a most interesting conversation on my
heavy water intercept wristwatch. *(BETTY is intensely
curious)* Prepare yourself for a shock, Betty. Lorelei spoke

the truth. Woof knew from the first. The man who says he's your uncle isn't. *(BETTY gasps)* He's The Fog. *(Another gasp)* He's in league with a beautiful but evil foreign agent. Countess Frederika.

BETTY. How do you know she's beautiful, Dan? *(DAN doesn't want to answer. Settles for—)*

DAN. We've met. *(MUSIC STING. BETTY looks into the audience, horrified. She has grasped the romantic implications)*

BETTY. But, Dan, if The Fog is impersonating Uncle Philo, where's Uncle Philo?

DAN. Good question.

BETTY. I'd rather hear a good answer. *(A terrible thought strikes DAN)*

DAN. Wait! Oh, no. Not that. They wouldn't dare.

BETTY. What?

DAN. I was thinking of what's under this room. *(Another gasp from BETTY)* The shark.

BETTY. The shark. The pirate. The robot. The Fog. No wonder this house is called Nightmare Castle.

DAN. It's no YMCA.

BETTY. If only your invisibility ring hadn't conked out.

DAN. The breaks.

MURDOCK. *(ENTERS from the cellar, to BETTY)* Ah, there you are, my dear.

DAN. *(To BETTY, stage whisper)* Act normal. *(Foolishly attempting to appear casual, BETTY crosses her legs, again. Forces a smile — only the smile is awkward. Grotesque, in fact.* [NOTE: Remember, MURDOCK is assuming DAN does not associate him with THE FOG]

MURDOCK. Enjoying your stay?

Betty. *(Blabbering)* Yes, yes, Uncle. Oh, yes. Yes, yes, yes. Yes, yes. Oh, yes. Yes. *(Crosses her legs again)*

Murdock. Splendid.

Dan. Looking for something, Professor?

Murdock. I'm looking for Lorelei. Have you seen the girl?

Lorelei. *(Enters Left)* Here I am, sir. *(Another of her stupid curtsies)*

Murdock. Where have you been?

Lorelei. *(Indicates Left)* Some "merchandise" was delivered.

Murdock. Never mind about that. I need you in the cellar. *(As MURDOCK and LORELEI speak, DAN and BETTY listen with interest, moving heads from side to side — like spectators at a tennis match)*

Lorelei. The cellar?

Murdock. There is work for you in the cellar. *(Gestures)* Don't waste time, Lorelei.

Lorelei. No, sir. *(She moves quickly for the cellar, speaks to DAN, sotto, as she passes)* I must speak with you.

Murdock. *(Shouts)* You're wasting time! *(LORELEI practically FLIES into the cellarway)*

Dan. What's in the cellar, Professor?

Murdock. I keep a shark for experimental purposes. He won't eat unless Lorelei feeds him.

Betty. Gosh.

Dan. I'd like to see that shark. I'm interested in aquatic creatures. I speak whale and a bit of porpoise.

Murdock. Unfortunately, I can't allow it. He doesn't like strangers. If you see a robot, don't be alarmed. It's quite harmless.

BETTY. I have seen it. It didn't seem harmless to me. It was uncontrollable.

MURDOCK. It's nothing but a big, overgrown toy. Now, if you'll excuse me. Feeding time. *(He EXITS)*

BETTY. *(Stands)* What's going on down there?

DAN. I intend to find out. *(DAN moves for the cellar. AN-YANKA, a gypsy girl in full Romany attire, ENTERS LEFT. Balkan accent)*

ANYANKA. I would like to wash my hands. Where can I wash my hands?

BETTY. Dan! *(DAN stops, turns. He and BETTY stare at the gypsy)*

ANYANKA. Something, maybe, is wrong?

BETTY. Who are you?

ANYANKA. Anyanka.

BETTY. Anyanka?

ANYANKA. How much did you have to pay Cap'n Scar? I don't trust him.

BETTY. I have no idea what you're talking about.

DAN. *(Quickly grasps the situation)* But I do.

NYOKA'S VOICE. *(OFFSTAGE; from hallway, RIGHT)* Yoo-hoo, Dan. Yoo-hoo.

ANYANKA. More merchandise?

BETTY. It's a neighbor.

ANYANKA. Neighbor? I, maybe, should make myself scarce. *(FLEES LEFT as NYOKA APPEARS in hallway, takes a step into the room. ANNOUNCER ENTERS radio studio, stands at mike)*

NYOKA. You'll think me a perfect ninny, but I forget to take along a flashlight. It's so terribly dark outside. A storm's on the way. I wonder, Dan, would you be good enough to escort me back to my isolated cottage?

DAN. Dan Daredevil never refuses the opportunity to perform a good deed.

NYOKA. One in a m llion. You live up to your reputation. *(Starts OUT)* The cliffs can be treacherous.

DAN. *(Moves after her)* This way, Woof.

ANNOUNCER. Woof. *(DAN is OUT. ANNOUNCER EXITS. BETTY is left alone and she doesn't like it)*

BETTY. *(Calls UPSTAGE)* Wait. I'm coming with you. *(She takes a step UPSTAGE as ANYANKA RETURNS)*

ANYANKA. Cap'n Scar said this house was safe. He didn't say anything about neighbors. *(Sits on the sofa)* What a wretched trip. The boat leaked and I got seasick. Still, anything's better than where I came from.

BETTY. *(Strongly)* I don't believe you're an American citizen.

ANYANKA. Of course I'm not. But I want to be. That's why I had to hire Cap'n Scar. *(CAP'N SCAR ENTERS LEFT)*

CAP'N SCAR. Did I hear my name?

ANYANKA. *(To CAP'N SCAR, indicates BETTY)* Who is she?

CAP'N SCAR. Probably a friend of the Professor's.

BETTY. I'm no such thing. I'm his niece. I'm someone's niece. *(Courageously)* I'm not afraid of you. I don't know who you are. I don't know why you wear that dumb costume. I do suspect this: You're running illegals into this country for a price.

CAP'N SCAR. I provide a service. Besides, they're not illegals.

ANYANKA. No, no, no.

BETTY. If they're not illegals, what are they? *(As AN-YANKA stands and she and CAP'N SCAR begin to sing, BETTY moves to chair at desk, sits) NOTE: [If desired, some EXTRA TRAVELLERS can APPEAR from LEFT and join in the number]*

[Music: TRAVELLERS WITHOUT PASSPORTS]

CAP'N SCAR.
OH, I AM LIKE A SPECIAL TRAVEL AGENT
SO COME TO ME AND I WILL PLAN YOUR TRIP.
BUT DON'T REQUEST A TRAIN, AND NEVER GO
    BY PLANE
I WELCOME YOU ABORAD MY SPECIAL SHIP.
YES, I PROVIDE A FRIENDLY LITTLE SERVICE
AND YOU MAY LEAVE YOUR COUNTRY FOR A
    PRICE.
IT'S TRUE I SOMETIMES HIDE THE PASSENGERS
    WHO RIDE
BUT CALLING THEM 'ILLEGALS' ISN'T NICE.
THEY ARE TRAVELLERS WITHOUT PASSPORTS
AND THEY HAVEN'T GOT A VISA TO THEIR
    NAME.
THEY ARE TRAVELLERS WITHOUT PASSPORTS
BUT THEY REACH THEIR DESTINATION JUST
    THE SAME.
NOW THE TIME HAS COME FOR PARTING
SOON THE ENGINE WILL BE STARTING
NOW WE'RE OUT IN THE ATLANTIC
AND THE OCEAN LOOKS GIGANTIC
THOUGH THE PASSENGERS ARE HIDDEN

AND THE CARGO IS FORBIDDEN
THEY WILL REACH THEIR DESTINATION JUST
  THE SAME!
HEY!
  ANYANKA.
OH, I CONFESS I'M JUST A SIMPLE GYPSY
BUT SUCH A LIFE'S A CONSTANT FREE-FOR-
  ALL.
I NEVER LEARNED TO TELL A FORTUNE VERY
  WELL
AND APRIL LAST, I BROKE MY CRYSTAL BALL.
AND SO I MADE A VISIT TO THE CAPTAIN
AND TOLD HIM, "THERE IS SOMETHING I
  MUST SAY.
I HAVE NO DOCUMENTS." HE SAID, "PLEASE,
  NO LAMENTS.
JUST CROSS MY PALM I'LL TAKE YOU ANYWAY."
WITH THOSE TRAVELLERS WITHOUT PASSPORTS
WHO JUST HAVEN'T GOT A VISA TO THEIR
  NAME.
WE WERE TRAVELLERS WITHOUT PASSPORTS
BUT WE REACHED OUR DESTINATION JUST
  THE SAME.
PEOPLE STARTED IN TO PRAY HARD
"PLEASE DON'T RUN INTO THE COAST GUARD."
WE WERE OUT UPON THE OCEAN
AND WE FELT A ROCKING MOTION
NOW, PLEASE PARDON MY KVETCHING,
BUT THE PASSENGERS WERE WRETCHING
BUT WE REACHED OUR DESTINATION JUST
  THE SAME!

CAP'N SCAR & ANYANKA.
(THEY/WE) WERE TRAVELLERS WITHOUT PASS-
    PORTS
AND (THEY/WE) DIDN'T HAVE A VISA TO (THEIR/
    OUR) NAME
(THEY/WE) WERE TRAVELLERS WITHOUT PASS-
    PORTS
BUT (THEY/WE) REACHED (THEIR/OUR) DES-
    TINATION JUST THE SAME.
ANYANKA.
SO IF YOU DEPART ALBANIA
CAP'N SCAR.
OR EVEN LITHUANIA
ANYANKA.
OR IF YOU LEAVE ROUMANIA
CAP'N SCAR.
OR MAYBE TRANSYLVANIA
ANYANKA.
IF YOU DEPART TASMANIA
CAP'N SCAR.
OR EVEN PENNSYLVANIA!
BOTH.
YOU WILL REACH YOUR DESTINATION JUST
    THE SAME!
HEY!

*(MRS. HERRINGBONE ENTERS from cellar, sees ANYANKA
and BETTY)*

MRS. HERRINGBONE. *(To CAP'N SCAR)* You fool!
CAP'N SCAR. *(Holds up the hook)* Watch what you say.

MRS. HERRINGBONE. *(Indicates BETTY)* The girl has seen you. She's heard you. She knows too much.

BETTY. *(Stands)* Lay one hand on me and you'll answer to Dan Daredevil.

MRS. HERRINGBONE. *(Mockingly)* Dan Daredevil. *(Puts her tongue between her teeth, makes a raspberry)*

ANYANKA. *(To CAP'N SCAR)* You said there'd be no trouble.

CAP'N SCAR. Nothing I can't handle. *(BETTY starts to run UPSTAGE, for the hallway)*

MRS. HERRINGBONE. Catch her! *(Fast, CAP'N SCAR zooms to the hallway and blocks BETTY'S escape)*

CAP'N SCAR. I won't lay a hand on you. *(Holds up hook)* It'll be a hook!

MRS. HERRINGBONE. Into the cellar.

BETTY. *(Backing away from CAP'N SCAR)* Stay away from me. *(BETTY continues to back away from the pirate and he continues to advance)*

CAP'N SCAR. You heard Mrs. Herringbone. What's it to be? The cellar or the hook? *(Having no choice, BETTY crosses to the cellar, pauses. She looks to audience and gives a helpless little scream, EXITS)*

MRS. HERRINGBONE. *(To ANYANKA)* You. Upstairs. All the way up. The attic. You'll find rooms. Take any one you want. Stay out of sight.

ANYANKA. I should, maybe, have stayed home. *(She EXITS into hallway, OFF)*

CAP'N SCAR. What are we going to do about that girl?

MRS. HERRINGBONE. We're not going to do anything. The shark will do it all. Same for Dan Daredevil. I've been waiting a long time to settle a score with him, *(As LIGHTS DIM, she ENTERS cellar. CAP'N SCAR FOLLOWS. ANNOUNCER ENTERS radio studio, stands at mike)*

ANNOUNCER. *(Script)* Well, fans, things are getting mighty chilly at Nightmare Castle. I hope Dan can win this one. And now, for all you Dan Daredevil fans with your personal decoder, here's tonight's message. Two words. *(Dramatic)* First word. B-7. *(Pause)* G-12. I'll repeat that. *(Repeats)* B-7. G-12. Second word. *(Pause)* A-6, D-3, J-9, S-14, Z-305. I'll repeat that. *(So fast no one could possibly get it)* A-6, D-3, J-9, S-14, Z-305. *(Important)* This message is not available to non-members of the Dan Daredevil Amazzzzzing Adventures Club. And save those Crunchy box tops for your invisibility ring and secret decoder — if you don't already have one. *(Ominous tone)* Meanwhile, back at Nightmare Castle ... *(PHILO runs INTO the room from the cellar. ANNOUNCER EXITS)*

PHILO. You won't get me! *(He darts behind the sofa. Running IN after him are: MURDOCK, CAP'N SCAR, MRS. HERRINGBONE, LORELEI)*

MURDOCK. You're only making things worse, Professor.

PHILO. That's what I want to do. Where's my niece? *(PHILO is not quite clearheaded)*

MURDOCK. *(To CAP'N SCAR)* That way. *(He points to in front of the sofa. CAP'N SCAR crosses. MURDOCK moves to in back of the sofa. A "pincher" movement. MURDOCK and CAP'N SCAR walk in exaggerated fashion — as if they didn't want PHILO to "hear" them. MRS. HERRINGBONE moves to chair in front of desk and re-positions it for good audience sightlines. LORELEI is close to another one of her "fits")*

Lorelei. Tell them what they want to know, Professor. It's the only way. No telling what they'll do if you don't tell.

Philo. Have to catch me first.

Murdock. No problem. *(To CAP'N SCAR) Now! (CAP'N SCAR jumps for PHILO. Same for MURDOCK. They get him. Pull the old man to the chair)*

Philo. Take your hands off me! Let me go. I won't tell you a thing!

Murdock. We'll see about that. *(They shove PHILO into the chair)* What controls the robot? What makes him obey? All Adam does is clank about the house.

Lorelei. Bumps into the furniture.

Mrs. Herringbone. He's useless.

Philo. You think I don't know what you're planning? If the robot fell into the wrong hands—

Mrs. Herringbone. It's easy enough to construct the things, but how do you *control* them? *(MURDOCK crosses to blackboard, points to his "calulations")*

Murdock. What's wrong with my calculations?

Philo. *(Looks)* Ha! If you follow those calculations, the only thing you'll come up with is Kool-Aid.

Murdock. *(Snarls)* Very funny, Professor.

Cap'n Scar. *(Snide)* Ha, ha.

Mrs. Herringbone. We're wasting time.

[Music: YOU'D BETTER TELL]

Murdock.
IF YOU DON'T WANT TO FIND YOUR COURAGE
SLOWLY DWINDLING INTO CRUMBS

Mrs. Herringbone.
IF YOU DON'T LIKE TO HEAR THE SOUND OF
NATIVES BEATING ON THEIR DRUMS
Cap'n Scar.
IF YOU WOULD HATE TO FIND YOU'RE IN THE
JUNGLE HANGING BY YOUR THUMBS
All Villains.
YOU'D BETTER TELL!
Philo.
I'LL NEVER TELL!
Murdock.
IF YOU DON'T WANT TO FIND YOUR SPIRIT QUICKLY
SHATTERED INTO GLASS
Mrs. Herringbone.
IF YOU DON'T LIKE THE SOUND OF RATTLE-
SNAKES THAT SLITHER THROUGH THE GRASS
Cap'n Scar.
IF YOU WOULD HATE TO BE ABANDONED IN A
ROOM OF LEAKING GAS
All Villains.
YOU'D BETTER TELL!
Philo.
I'LL NEVER TELL!
All Villains.
OH, THERE ARE WAYS TO MAKE YOU SPEAK
OF GETTING ALL THE INFORMATION THAT WE
SEEK
YES, THERE ARE WAYS AND THERE ARE MEANS
Murdock.
SO IF YOU'RE SMART YOU'LL OPEN UP AND SPILL
THE BEANS.

Murdock.
IF YOU DON'T WANT TO FIND YOUR NERVES
    BECOMING TANGLED IN A KNOT
Mrs. Herringbone.
IF YOU DON'T LIKE TO WALK UPON A BED OF
    COALS ALL SIZZLING HOT
Cap'n Scar.
IF YOU WOULD HATE TO FIND YOU'RE BEING
    SALT-AND-PEPPERED IN A POT
Lorelei.   *(Pleading with PHILO)*
YOU'D BETTER TELL!
Philo.
I'LL NEVER TELL!
Lorelei. *(Spoken during vamp after first chorus ends)* Oh,
please. Professor, you must save yourself! I beg of you!
Tell them what they want to know!
Philo. *(Spoken)* Never! Never!
Cap'n Scar.
IF YOU DON'T WANT TO FIND YOUR COURAGE
    SLOWLY MELTING FROM THE STRAIN
Murdock.
IF YOU DON'T LIKE THE THOUGHT OF NEEDLES
    AND EXCRUCIATING PAIN
Mrs. Herringbone.
IF YOU WOULD HATE TO HAVE EXPERIMENTS
    PERFORMED UPON YOUR BRAIN
Villains & Lorelei.
YOU'D BETTER TELL!
Philo.
I'LL NEVER TELL!
Cap'n Scar.
IF YOU DON'T WANT TO FIND YOUR SPIRIT AND
    YOUR WILL BEGIN TO BREAK

Murdock.
IF YOU DON'T LIKE THE THOUGHT OF CON-
CRETE SHOES AND SINKING IN A LAKE
Mrs. Herringbone.
IF YOU WOULD HATE TO FIND YOU'RE
FASTENED TO A BURNING WOODEN STAKE
Villains & Lorelei.
YOU'D BETTER TELL!
Philo.
I'LL NEVER TELL!
All Villains.
OH, THERE ARE WAYS TO MAKE YOU SPEAK
OF GETTING ALL THE INFORMATION THAT WE
SEEK
YES, THERE IS TIME, THE NIGHT IS YOUNG
Mrs. Herringbone.
WE'LL FIND THAT STUBBORN CAT THAT SEEMS
TO HAVE YOUR TONGUE.
Cap'n Scar.
IF YOU DON'T WANT TO FIND YOUR NERVES ARE
CRUMBLING JUST A LITTLE BIT
Murdock.
IF YOU DON'T LIKE THE THOUGHT OF BEING
TOSSED INTO A VIPER PIT
Mrs. Herringbone.
IF YOU WOULD HATE TO FIND YOU'RE BARBE -
QUED AND ROASTING ON A SPIT
Villains & Lorelei.
YOU'D BETTER TELL!
Philo.
I'LL NEVER TELL!

All Villains.
JUST LET THE INFORMATION SLIP
JUST TAKE THAT BUTTON OFF YOUR LIP
YOU'D BETTER TELL!
YOU'D BETTER TELL!
(Thinking fast, PHILO points DOWN LEFT)

Philo. It's Adam! The robot! *(ALL look. PHILO uses this distraction to dart back into the cellar)*

Lorelei. Run, Professor! *(OTHERS turn)*

Cap'n Scar. I'll get him. *(He grabs LORELEI'S wrist and pulls her into the cellar)*

Mrs. Herringbone. The old fool has gotten his senses back.

Murdock. He's been playing us for dummies!

Mrs. Herringbone. *(Points to window)* Look! Out on the cliff.

Murdock. What?

Mrs. Herringbone. I saw something.

Murdock. *(Looks)* Your imagination.

Mrs. Herringbone. I tell you I saw something. *(She crosses to the window, looks out. At the same time, BETTY struggles to pull herself INTO VIEW at the EXTREME DOWN RIGHT cliff. In one hand she carries a lighted lantern or flashlight)* I was right. It's the old man's niece. *(MURDOCK steps to window, looks. SOUND: HOWLING WIND. BETTY puts her hand over the light's beam, takes it away. Repeats business. Faster, slowly)*

Murdock. How did she manage to get to the cliff?

Mrs. Herringbone. It doesn't matter. Can't you see what she's doing!

Murdock. Hmmmmmm. Looks like dots and dashes.

Mrs. Herringbone. *(Scoffs)* Dots and dashes. *(Livid)* Morse code!

Murdock. She must be stopped!

Mrs. Herringbone. I'll stop her. Never fear. *(MRS. HERRINGBONE darts INTO the cellar)*

Murdock. *(Continues to look out the window)* Who would have thought the girl had so much spunk? *(COUNTESS FREDERIKA SLINKS from behind the dressing screen [or, she can APPEAR in the hallway], strikes a pose)*

Frederika. I would.

Murdock. *(Sees her)* Countess Frederika!

Frederika. I hope I am not too late to salvage the damage. Imbecile. *(Steps into room)*

Murdock. I will soon have the information.

Frederika. You've been telling me that for weeks. Cretin.

Murdock. The old man is a tough nut to crack.

Frederika. I'll not only crack him, I'll smash him. All men are turnips. *(As they converse, MRS. HERRINGBONE APPEARS on the cliff, struggles to pull BETTY down)*

Murdock. These unnamed foreign powers you work for — who are they? *(ANNOUNCER APPEARS at radio studio microphone)*

Frederika. That needn't concern you. *(As FREDERIKA and MURDOCK talk, BETTY struggles with MRS. HER-RINGBONE, who pulls a knife and attempts to stab her. BETTY whacks the woman on the head with the flashlight or gives her a shove. MRS. HERRINGBONE "falls" from the cliff and OUT OF SIGHT)*

Announcer. *(Imitating the falling MRS. HERRING-BONE. A descending wail)* Auuuuuuuuuuuuuuuuuuugh.

(BETTY looks below)

Betty. Oops. *(BETTY climbs from the rock and OUT)*

Murdock. Your coming here might prove dangerous. Aren't you forgetting him?

Frederika. Who?

Announcer. Woof, woof, woof. *(FREDERIKA smiles, recognizing the bark)*

Frederika. Aha! It's Woof, The Wonder Dog. Bring me the Professor. *(ANNOUNCER EXITS)*

Murdock. But Dan Daredevil?

Frederika. *(Hard)* Don't argue. *(MURDOCK knows better than to argue with her. EXITS into cellar. FREDERIKA fluffs at her hair. Turns UPSTAGE to face the approaching DAN DAREDEVIL, strikes a seductive pose)*

Dan's Voice. *(OFFSTAGE, from hallway)* Attaboy, Woof. *(He APPEARS. Sees FREDERIKA, and he's not surprised. There's an "attraction")*

Dan. So, Countess. We meet again.

Frederika. Yes.

Dan. You're a beautiful woman.

Frederika. Thank you.

Dan. But you're evil. *(He moves toward her)*

Frederika. A matter of opinion.

Dan. I might have known you'd be mixed up in this.

Frederika. I'm pleased that you haven't forgotten me.

Dan. I could never forget that night in Pasadena *(Pause)* You stole my wallet.

Frederika. Ah, yes. the night of the Ambassador's reception. The night he "disappeared." I didn't steal your wallet, Dan. I took it because I wanted a memento of our first meeting. Forgive me, but I am a sentimental creature. *(Unable to control herself, she grabs DAN and gives him a Hollywood smooch)*

DAN. *(Ignores the smooch)* If only you'd turn your talents to good instead of evil.

FREDERIKA. Evil is relative.

DAN. No relative of mine.

FREDERIKA. We could be rich, Dan. Richer than Midas. We could be powerful. More powerful than Alexander the Great. I'm not like other women. You're not like other men. Join with me, Dan. Together, the world is ours.

DAN. I'd sooner eat junk food.

FREDERIKA. *(Scheming, scheming)* You're angry with me.

DAN. I hate to see potential wasted. Mind telling me what the game is!

FREDERIKA. Why not? It would amuse me. An army of robots. *Capable of conquering the world.*

DAN. I should have guessed. It's a foul scheme. *(Chest out)* Fortunately, I'm here to stop you. And The Fog.

FREDERIKA. The Fog is of no consequence. A mere henchman. Will you throw in with me?

DAN. Don't insult my intelligence.

FREDERIKA. Don't force me to use the death-ray gun.

DAN. I'm not afraid of your death-ray gun. I'm not afraid of your decimator. I'm not afraid of your cyclotrode. Do your worst. *(She holds out her hand. Sweetly—)*

FREDERIKA. You gave me this ring, didn't you, Daredevil Dan? *(DAN stoops to look)*

DAN. Ring? I don't think so. *(FREDERIKA blows on the ring and some powder-like substance hits DAN smack in the face. he recoils, sprawls back on the sofa)* Ugh! Immobilizing gas. It's gotten Woof, too. *(He gasps for breath, passes out)*

FREDERIKA. Sorry, Dan. I cannot allow you to interfere with my plans. You must be "eliminated." You had your chance.

[Music: STRANGE MUSIC IN MY HEART]

FREDERIKA.
I CONFESS THAT I AM IN A QUANDARY
WHEN IT COMES TO DAN, I'M PUZZLED AND
    PERPLEXED.
THAT MAN THAT I SHOULD KILL
STILL GIVES ME SUCH A THRILL
SO WHY ELMININATE HIM WHEN I REALLY
    WANT TO DATE HIM?
WHEN HE'S NEAR I START TO HEAR A SYMPHONY
EV'RY INSTRUMENT IS SWEET AND CLEAR
SO, NOW MUSIC, MAESTRO, PLEASE,
IN SEVERAL DIFF'RENT KEYS
AND LET'S FACE THE MUSIC, MY DEAR.
HE WALKS IN THE ROOM AND THE MUSIC
    BEGINS
TRUMPETS AT FIRST, THEN VIOLINS
THE SOUND OF HIS VOICE MAKES AN
    ORCHESTRA START
STRANGE MUSIC IN MY HEART.
I SOON HEAR A PICCOLO WHEN HE APPEARS

CYMBALS AND DRUMS CRASH IN MY EARS
AND SUDDENLY TROMBONES AND CLARINETS
  START
STRANGE MUSIC IN MY HEART.
OH, SOMETIMES I THINK I HATE HIM
I'M THROUGH WITH THESE ONE-WAY AFFAIRS
BUT WHEN I HEAR CASTANETS CLICKING
I WANT TO PLAY MUSICAL CHAIRS.
AT TIMES I JUST WISH THAT THE CONCERT
  WOULD END
BUT WHAT'S THE USE? I CAN'T PRETEND.
SO, STRIKE UP THE BAND AND PLEASE TELL
  THEM TO START
STRANGE MUSIC IN MY HEART.
HE WALKS THROUGH THE DOOR AND I SOON
  HEAR A TUNE
BAGPIPES AT FIRST, THEN A BASSOON
THE SOUND OF HIS VOICE MAKES ACCORDIANS
  START
STRANGE MUSIC IN MY HEART.
I HEAR UKELELES WHEN HE COMES IN SIGHT
OBOES AND FLUTES SING THROUGH THE NIGHT
AND SUDDENLY FIFTY HARMONICAS START
STRANGE MUSIC IN MY HEART.
OH, SOMETIMES I THINK I HATE HIM
OUR ROMANCE IS FAR FROM IDEAL
BUT WHEN I HEAR TAMBOURINES SHAKING
I WANT TO RING MY GLOCKENSPIEL.
THE TUBAS AND XYLOPHONES START UP A
  WALTZ
I JUST ADORE VIENNESE SCHMALTZ

"ICH LIEBE DICH, LIEBCHEN," PLEASE TELL
  THEM TO START
STRANGE MUSIC IN MY HEART.
OH, SOMETIMES I THINK I HATE HIM
SUCH CONFLICT! OH, WHAT SHOULD I DO?
BUT WHEN THOSE MARACAS ARE SHAKING
I MUST TOOT UPON MY KAZOO.
AT TIMES I JUST WISH THAT THE CONCERT
  WOULD END
BUT WHAT'S THE USE? I CAN'T PRETEND.
SO, STRIKE UP THE BAND AND PLEASE TELL
  THEM TO START
STRANGE MUSIC IN MY HEART.
(MURDOCK drags IN PHILO from cellar)

MURDOCK. Here's the Professor.

PHILO. I'll never talk. Never!

FREDERIKA. Never is a long time.

MURDOCK. This is another job for — The Fog! *(Darts
behind dressing screen)*

CAP'N SCAR'S VOICE. *(OFFSTAGE)* Get in there, you!
(BETTY is shoved INTO the room. CAP'N SCAR behind her)

BETTY. Uncle!

PHILO. Betty!

FREDERIKA. Scar!

CAP'N SCAR. Countess!

FREDERIKA. The Fog didn't say you were here.

CAP'N SCAR. Maybe he don't want you to know.

FREDERIKA. Typical. *(Looks to screen)* I'll deal with him
later. *(Nervously, the screen begins to "shake." MURDOCK is
terrified of FREDERIKA'S wrath)* Who's the girl?

CAP'N SCAR. The Professor's niece.

FREDERIKA. Excellent.

CAP'N SCAR. She pushed Herringbone off the cliff. She's laying on the beach with a leg cramp. *(DAN is still unconscious, sprawled on the sofa)*

BETTY. Dan! What have you done to Dan!

FREDERIKA. Immobilizing gas.

BETTY. Oh, no! *(Looks)* Woof, too.

FREDERIKA. Professor Murdock, will you tell me how to control the robot or not?

PHILO. Not.

FREDERIKA. In that case, you leave me no choice. *(All business)* The girl. *(CAP'N SCAR grabs BETTY)*

BETTY. No, no, let me go.

CAP'N SCAR. Ha, ha.

PHILO. *(Holds up shackles)* If only my hands were free. *(FREDERIKA moves to UPSTAGE side of rug and "lifts" the trapdoor)*

FREDERIKA. *(To CAP'N SCAR)* What are you waiting for? *(CAP'N SCAR pulls BETTY to the trap. She continues to struggle)*

BETTY. If only Dan hadn't been gassed!

PHILO. *(Laments)* If only I weren't so weak. Haven't eaten in days. *(At this point, FREDERIKA, BETTY and CAP'N SCAR are behind the rug, looking "down." PHILO is by the desk and DAN remains, out cold, on the sofa. MURDOCK behind screen)*

FREDERIKA. Say goodbye to your niece, Professor.

PHILO. Goodbye.

CAP'N SCAR. Plip, plop.

PHILO. You did your best, Betty. Thank you.

BETTY. Don't tell her anything, Uncle Philo. Dan says

she's a foreign agent.

PHILO. I figured as much.

FREDERIKA. Throw her to the shark! *(BETTY screams as CAP'N SCAR starts to shove)*

PHILO. Wait! I'll tell.

MURDOCK. *(Coming from behind the screen, back INTO his THE FOG persona)* He's come to his senses, Countess.

FREDERIKA. No thanks to you. *(Sizes up costume)* That disguise is ridiculous.

MURDOCK. I think it has flair.

PHILO. Don't harm Betty...

FREDERIKA. I'm waiting, Professor. I'm impatient. *(Suddenly, PHILO is alert and informative. As if nothing at all were out of line, he gives the desired information. He could be addressing a college class)*

PHILO. *(Out to audience)* Once the robot hears the correct frequency, he will carry out orders via mental telepathy. Or, in his case, "metal" telepathy.

MURDOCK. *Metal* telepathy! I should have guessed.

FREDERIKA. You mean it "hears" the frequency, and then it's controlled by the brain energy of the sender?

PHILO. Something like that.

FREDERIKA. What is the frequency?

PHILO. The male voice. The sender must sing out a secure B over C in the top range and never waver.

FREDERIKA. That's impossible.

PHILO. I was able to do it. I trained myself. But I caught cold in the cellar. I'm hoarse.

MURDOCK. Countess, do you realize what this means? If there's a man alive who can sing B over C, he can control the robot. He can make it smash and kill. Conquer and rule.

CAP'N SCAR. Where are we going to find a guy like that? *(Instantly, DAN springs awake and sits up. Lets go with a long, high, ascending note)* NOTE: [Supposedly, this is the controlling B over C from a male voice. Just make sure the "sound" is loooooooong, loooooooooud and fuuuuuuuny]

BETTY. Dan!

DAN. Don't worry, Betty. I'm back to my old self! *(To prove his point, he leaps over the sofa back)*

MURDOCK. *(To VILLAINS)* Run! *(MURDOCK, CAP'N SCAR, FREDERIKA cross, on the run, to the hallway. ADAM THE ROBOT, looking as angry and as powerful as it can, whirls INTO VIEW. Its arms flail about, eager to strike at anything in its way)*

CAP'N SCAR. The robot!

FREDERIKA. It's attacking!

MURDOCK. It's gone crazy!

FREDERIKA. Daredevil is controlling it.

MURDOCK. The cellar! *(MURDOCK, CAP'N SCAR, FREDERIKA hurry to the cellar. THE ROBOT follows after them. DAN zooms to the cellar to block the escape. PHILO moves to BETTY. MURDOCK struggles with DAN, but DAN knocks him out. CAP'N SCAR struggles with DAN, gets knocked out. THE ROBOT whirls about dizzily)*

FREDERIKA. *(Hands up in surrender)* You win, Dan Daredevil. *(ROBOT stops. NYOKA APPEARS in the hallway, from RIGHT. She carries a revolver. Her manner, now, is direct and professional)* NOTE: [Another opportunity for an EXTRA or two as "government agents." Trench coats and hats. Weapons]

NYOKA. I'll take charge now, Dan.

BETTY. Mrs. Sterling!

DAN. Nyoka Sterling is a government agent. She told me she's been watching Nightmare Castle for weeks.

NYOKA. Illegal immigrants. *(To DAN)* I figured now was the time to move in. I saw your signal on the cliff.

BETTY. That was me trying to attract the Coast Guard. Look for a woman with a leg cramp.

FREDERIKA. *(To unconscious MURDOCK)* Illegal immigrants? *(Contemptuous)* Amateur!

CAP'N SCAR. *(Lifting his head from the floor)* You've got no proof. *(LORELEI ENTERS from cellar)*

LORELEI. *(To NYOKA)* Look in the attic. You'll find all the proof you need. NOTE: [For a silly laugh at this point, LORELEI might carry in an inflated rubber "shark" and stroke it as if it were a kitten. Such an item is readily available from many joke/novelty shops]

DAN. *(To NYOKA, dramatic)* You don't know the half of it, Nyoka. Evil plans were afoot in Nightmare Castle. Evil plans to conquer the world.

NYOKA. I'll want a full report.

DAN. You'll have it.

FREDERIKA. As an enemy, I despise you, Dan Daredevil. But as a man — ?

BETTY. *(Admiringly)* Oh, Dan. There's nothing you can't do.

PHILO. You saved my life, Dan.

DAN. *(Chest out, hands on hips)* Think nothing of it, Professor. The whole purpose of my life is watching out for the little guy. No doubt about it. This has been another *amazzzzzing* adventure! *(ANNOUNCER ENTERS radio studio, "woofing" a few times to let us know WOOF is alive and kicking.*

The DAREDEVILETTES also ENTER studio. ANNOUNCER and DAREDEVILETTES move into room, stand LEFT. DAN moves DOWN CENTER, BETTY joins him. MURDOCK and CAP'N remain out. FREDERIKA remains with her hands up)

[Music: THE DAN DAREDEVIL CREED
AND
FINALE ACT TWO]

ANNOUNCER. Woof! Woof! *(MUSIC in and under)*

DAN. Woof, The Wonder Dog, joins me in a special message for all of our friends and listeners out there in Radio Land.

ANNOUNCER. Woof! Woof!

DAN. If you try to be like Dan Daredevil, your parents and brothers and sisters and friends and The Girl Next Door and your teachers and your coaches and your teammates and your school and everybody will be proud of you and you'll be proud of yourself, too!

ANNOUNCER. Woof! Woof! *(DAN DAREDEVIL THEME MUSIC begins under)*

DAN. So join me now as we recite The Dan Daredevil Creed: *(ENTIRE CAST recites CREED with DAN)* "I dedicate my life to the protection of all my countrymen, wherever they may be. My battle is against evil. The whole purpose of my life is watching out for the little guy. Indivisible and with liberty and justice for all!"

ANNOUNCER. Woof! Woof!

[Reprise: DAN DAREDEVIL THEME SONG]

ALL.
WHO IS EV'RYBODY'S HERO?
DAN DAREDEVIL BRAVE AND BOLD.
GALLANT, LOYAL AND COURAGEOUS
HE'S THE INSPIRATION OF THE NATION.
STANDING TALL FOR TRUTH AND HONOR
EACH INJUSTICE HE'LL DESTROY.
HE'S OUR FAV'RITE SON, HE IS "NUMBER ONE"
HE'S AMERICA'S PRIDE AND JOY.
HE'S AMERICA'S PRIDE AND JOY!

END OF SPOOF

PRODUCTION NOTES

ON STAGE, ACT ONE: Standing radio microphone, cutout of large rock. Stairs or step unit (optional), standing blackboard, desk with two (2) chairs, suitcase with hand microphone, head phones. Dressing screen, table behind the screen. Sofa or chaise lounge, small table. Window, rug. Optional stage dressing.

BROUGHT ON: Radio script (ANNOUNCER), cardboard cutout of small plane (placed prior to opening of Act One), goggles, *starched* aviator scarves (DAN and BETTY), blueprints (MURDOCK). Tin cans or cups on a string (ANNOUNCER), chalk, whip (MURDOCK—in desk).

Hook hand (CAP'N SCAR), crutch, arm sling (DAN), letter in envelope (BETTY), small basket covered with checkered napkin (NYOKA), chains or shackles, fake beard (PHILO), flashlight (MRS. HERRINGBONE).

BROUGHT ON, ACT TWO: Basket (NYOKA), wristwatch (DAN), lantern or flashlight (BETTY), ring (FREDERIKA), knife (MRS. HERRINGBONE), revolver (NYOKA).

SOUND

Various effects to establish opening of radio episode:
Scream, gunfire, rushing train, insane laughter, explosion, police whistle (can be cut). Humming of airplane
motor, howling wind.

COSTUMES

As indicated in the script. The time frame is anywhere
from 1945 to 1952. You don't have to be completely in
period, although period hairstyles for the women will
prove atmospheric. Suit and tie for ANNOUNCER,
MURDOCK.

THE ROBOT

If you can use your imagination and come up with something wonderfully ridiculous go for it. It will get a BIG
laugh. Or, consider this: ADAM wears an old dark suit or
tuxedo. White gloves, a bathing cap with chinstrap painted white or silver [or a silver or white "helmet"]. The
actor's face is also painted silver or white, but the lips are
black. Dark glasses. A metal plug is stuck in the
thing's mouth.

IMMOBILIZING RING

The powder isn't necessary and the "effect" is covered by Dan's line, "Ugh! Immobilizing gas." However, if you want something visual it works this way — Countess has some powder [talc] in her clinched hand and when Dan stoops to the ring, she turns her fist upward, opens it and blows out the powder.

FLEXIBLE CASTING

If you want a smaller cast, consider this — DAREDEVILETTES might double. For example, #1 might play LORELEI, #2 might portray NYOKA, #3 COUNTESS FREDERIKA or ANYANKA. One might double, two, or all three. You might delete one or two of the vocalists. Or, you might even use male actor(s), or mix them up, in which case the vocalists become the DAREDEVILS.

If you want a larger cast think about using EXTRAS as "travellers without passports." And one or more as government agents when NYOKA appears near the finale.

ABOUT THE SET

The set is simplicity itself. Just the few items mentioned for the purposes of blocking. Since we are supposedly "hearing" the action instead of actually seeing it, nothing more is required. Also, it'll prove funny. However, if you have the resources for a realistic set — walls, curtains, doorways, doors, by all means go this route.

THE CLIFF ROCK: Helps if there is a small platform behind the cutout, so actors can "climb" into view.

RADIO STATION: A few items might be added. For example, a sign that lights up and says: ON AIR. An advertising poster for CRUNCHY CHEWS, or a large picture of DAN DAREDEVIL with WOOF, the Wonder Dog.

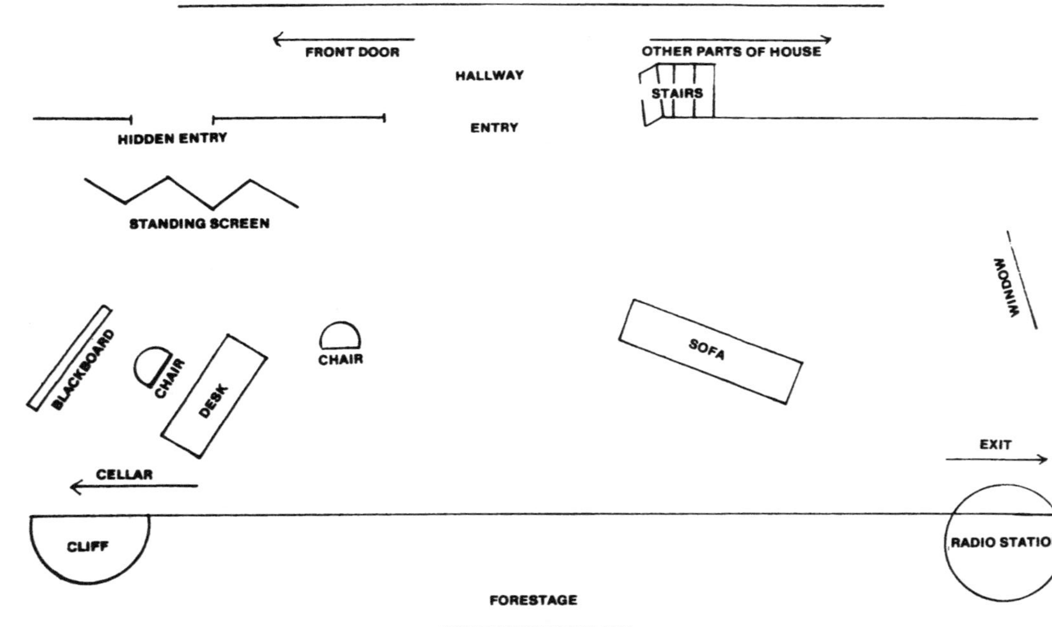

FORESTAGE

SUGGESTED SETTING FOR
"THE AMAZING ADVENTURES OF DAN DAREDEVIL"

OTHER TITLES AVAILABLE FROM BAKER'S PLAYS

COPIES

Brad Slaight

Dramatic Comedy, Jr. High/High Schools / 2m, 6f

An an orientation camp for new teenage clones, teens are sent to "Camp I.M.U" fresh from the lab to make a transition into the world of the "Originals" who have ordered them made. The newest "Copy" (a word they prefer to "clone") to arrive is a very bright and positive teenager named Michael who soon realizes what the other copies in his cottage have known for awhile – that their stay at the camp is much longer than they had thought. Michael befriends a rebellious Copy named Melissa, who does not get along with her Original and refuses to change her attitude in order to please her. She informs Michael, and the other Copies, that she is going to escape from the camp and fight for what she calls "copy rights". This is a story right out of tomorrow's headlines. Not good at math? Have a clone of yourself made from your own DNA, but gifted in math to do your problems for you. Need a spare part for the future? Your clone is a walking talking parts store. *Copies* explores the heart and soul of clones, bred specifically to do all those things you don't want to do

BAKERSPLAYS.COM

www.ingramcontent.com/pod-product-compliance
Lightning Source LLC
Chambersburg PA
CBHW070642120726
47909CB00004B/1547

* 9 7 8 0 8 7 4 4 0 0 9 5 3 *